S0-AZW-014

Alec swept Marissa into his arms, his mouth coming down on hers.

Yes. Yes! Marissa wound her arms around him and kissed him as if her very life had been given back to her.

Because it had.

Everything within her cried out for this moment. For at this moment, he was hers completely.

And then came the urgent cry.

"The baby," she whispered, her breath heavy against his cheek.

"Yours or mine?"

"Yours." Marissa was already backing away. "I'd better go see what she needs."

He could only nod, trying to pull himself together.

What had he almost gone and done? If his daughter hadn't cried out just then, heaven knows what would have happened.

Dear Reader,

This April, let Silhouette Romance shower you with treats. We've got must-read miniseries, bestselling authors and tons of happy endings!

The nonstop excitement begins with Marie Ferrarella's contribution to BUNDLES OF JOY. A single dad finds himself falling for his live-in nanny—who's got a baby of her own. So when a cry interrupts a midnight kiss, the question sure to be asked is *Your Baby or Mine?*

TWINS ON THE DOORSTEP, a miniseries about babies who bring love to the most unsuspecting couples, begins with *The Sheriff's Son*. Beloved author Stella Bagwell weaves a magical tale of secrets and second chances.

Also set to march down the aisle this month is the second member of THE SINGLE DADDY CLUB. Donna Clayton, winner of the prestigious Holt Medallion, brings you the story of a desperate daddy and the pampered debutante who becomes a *Nanny in the Nick of Time*.

SURPRISE BRIDES, a series about unexpected weddings, continues with Laura Anthony's *Look-Alike Bride*. This classic amnesia plot line has a new twist: Everyone believes a plain Jane is really a Hollywood starlet— including the actress's ex-fiancé!

Rounding out the month is the heartwarming *A Wife for Doctor Sam* by Phyllis Halldorson, the story of a small town doctor who's vowed never to fall in love again. And Sally Carleen's *Porcupine Ranch*, about a housekeeper who knows nothing about keeping house, but knows exactly how to keep her sexy boss happy!

Enjoy!

Melissa Senate
Senior Editor
Silhouette Romance

Please address questions and book requests to:
Silhouette Reader Service
U.S.: 3010 Walden Ave., P.O. Box 1325, Buffalo, NY 14269
Canadian: P.O. Box 609, Fort Erie, Ont. L2A 5X3

Marie Ferrarella

YOUR BABY OR MINE?

Silhouette
ROMANCE™
Published by Silhouette Books
America's Publisher of Contemporary Romance

If you purchased this book without a cover you should be aware
that this book is stolen property. It was reported as "unsold and
destroyed" to the publisher, and neither the author nor the
publisher has received any payment for this "stripped book."

To Barbara Benedict,
for showing me a picture of Christopher

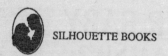 SILHOUETTE BOOKS

ISBN 0-373-19216-9

YOUR BABY OR MINE?

Copyright © 1997 by Marie Rydzynski-Ferrarella

All rights reserved. Except for use in any review, the reproduction
or utilization of this work in whole or in part in any form by any
electronic, mechanical or other means, now known or hereafter
invented, including xerography, photocopying and recording, or in
any information storage or retrieval system, is forbidden without
the written permission of the editorial office, Silhouette Books,
300 East 42nd Street, New York, NY 10017 U.S.A.

All characters in this book have no existence outside the imagination of
the author and have no relation whatsoever to anyone bearing the same
name or names. They are not even distantly inspired by any individual
known or unknown to the author, and all incidents are pure invention.

This edition published by arrangement with Harlequin Books S.A.

® and TM are trademarks of Harlequin Books S.A., used under license.
Trademarks indicated with ® are registered in the United States Patent
and Trademark Office, the Canadian Trade Marks Office and in other
countries.

Printed in U.S.A.

MARIE FERRARELLA

lives in Southern California. She describes herself as the tired mother of two overenergetic children and the contented wife of one wonderful man. This RITA Award-winning author is thrilled to be following her dream of writing full-time.

Dearest Readers,

I can't remember a time when I didn't love babies. All except for my brother Michael, but hey, he replaced me as the center of my parents' universe, and besides, he cried for the first two years. By the time my brother Mark came along, I was back on the baby bandwagon.

There is just something about babies—all babies—that makes me melt. Even energetic ones, and heaven knows I've had my share of those. The only reason I was brave enough to try for a second child after Jessica, who leapt off coffee tables, tried to fly and insisted on galloping on all fours in public, was because I didn't think God would do that to me twice. I figured my second child would be calm. Little did I realize that God has a sense of humor. Child number two made child number one look as if she were standing still most of the time. Nik bit through soda cans before he could walk, toppled mannequins in department stores—he thought they were big Barbie dolls—and once, at the age of two, unhooked my bra in the middle of a major toy store when he grabbed me by my blouse! Served me right for having a bra with a front clasp! There are bits and pieces of Jess and Nik in all the children I write about—children like Christopher in *Your Baby or Mine?* Despite what they put me through, I am still hopelessly hooked on babies and kids of all ages. I think, if you read my books, you might come away with that impression. You wouldn't be wrong.

As always, I thank you for reading and I hope I succeed in entertaining you.

Love,

Marie Ferrarella

Chapter One

He hated being late. It was one of those traits that he had always thought was rude in others and unforgivable in himself. But in the past few months, being late had seemed to become his inevitable fate. It was as if he was doomed to constantly be running behind every deadline, every event in his life.

It had been that way since last April. Twelve impossibly long months. A year.

A year in which Alec Beckett felt as if he were trapped in the last few minutes of an old war movie he'd once seen where the hero was running along the railroad tracks, trying to catch a train that would take him to freedom.

No matter what he did, that train just seemed to be getting farther and farther away from him.

And it had just gotten worse. Ellen had up and quit on him without so much as a full day's notice. She was the third nanny to leave in a year, if you didn't count the one he'd fired. It seemed that he was having no better luck in picking nannies than he was having in catching up.

"Not your fault, Andrea."

Alec looked down at the baby tucked against his chest. When she stared at him with those wide, green eyes, he sometimes had the feeling that his daughter could intuit things, that she knew exactly what he was thinking and reacted to it. Never mind that she was only a little more than a year old and had trouble feeding herself without sharing the contents of her spoon with her curly blond hair. She could see into his very soul.

"I just want you to know that. None of this is any of your fault. Everything just looks as if it's falling apart, but it's not. We're going to get through this, you and me. Don't you doubt that for a minute. Daddy's going to get his act together any day now."

He said it with enough feeling to almost convince himself.

Andrea smiled at the sound of her father's voice and uttered something unintelligible in response that he took to be agreement. His daughter's smile never ceased to uplift him. Andrea was the single being his whole world revolved around these days. Now that Christine was gone.

The small parking lot behind him was crowded with cars, family vehicles mostly, attesting to the fact that the people who were attending the session had probably already arrived.

He'd meant to leave work early, but then Rex had cornered him in the hallway, desperate for some data that was supposed to be delivered to a buyer by tomorrow noon. That set him back considerably. Rather than be early, Alec had wound up being half an hour late.

"Boy, this being both mom and dad business doesn't get any easier with time, does it?" He looked down at Andrea ruefully as he hurried up the five cement steps to the squat, new building where such warm and nurturing-sounding classes as Family Planning and Baby Gamboling were held regularly. The class he was rushing to was called Baby and Me. "I know, I know, you don't have anything to compare it to. But it'll get better, I promise. There's a lot of room for improvement here."

And improvement was what he was bent on. It was what had led him to sign up for the class in the first place. It would have been the kind of thing that Christine would have done, had she had the opportunity.

He'd hardly had proper time to mourn her. One moment, he was a widower, the next, the father of a tiny baby girl who was being placed in his arms. There'd been no time for tears. No time for anything except seeing to Andrea's needs and working.

It was only in the middle of the night that time seemed to stretch out endlessly, like a line that was plumbed down to infinity.

It had been a year and he had gone on with his life, but it wasn't easy. Alec kept his days so filled with work that there was no opportunity for grief, no opportunity for thought. Andrea saw to it that at least part of his evenings were busy. And all the while, Alec kept his emotions at arm's length until he could deal with them.

If ever.

"No music," he murmured to Andrea as he pulled open one of the double doors leading into the building.

The Baby and Me class was supposed to take place on the ground floor, first room to the left, just around the corner. If class was in session, he thought that there would be some sort of children's songs floating through the air.

"That's a good sign. Maybe we're not as late as I thought."

He wasn't sure why he thought there should be music coming from a Baby and Me class, he just did.

Truth of it was, he didn't know what to expect from such a class, only that attending it would be a good thing for

Andrea. He wanted her to grow up healthy and happy, and he wanted to compare notes with other parents to see if he was doing things right.

Maybe someone here would know where he could find a reputable nanny at a moment's notice. God knows he was at his wit's end.

With Ellen quitting yesterday evening and a meeting he absolutely had to attend this morning, Alec had turned to his mother in desperation and prevailed upon her to watch Andrea for the day.

Alec smiled to himself. Roberta Beckett wasn't the kind of woman Norman Rockwell had envisioned when he'd been painting all of those warm scenarios of hearth and home and loving grandmothers. She wasn't anyone's idea of the typical grandmother, which wasn't surprising since she hadn't been a typical mother, either. She didn't even answer to "Mother," only to "Roberta."

That change had come about almost fifteen years ago. Roberta had suddenly felt too young to have a fifteen-year-old son. Adjustments had to be made. Since he couldn't get younger, she did. She'd ceased being "Mother" and became "Roberta," falling somewhere between a sophisticated older sister and an eccentric aunt.

Sometimes, Alec thought, he really missed saying the word mother.

He looked at Andrea. So would she, he thought.

That was why he had to make it up to her. And attending this class was as good a way as any to begin. He meant to do all the things with his daughter that Christine no longer could. And all the things that Roberta had never done with him. He meant to give Andrea a stable family life, even if he was the only one in her family.

Hell of a way to start out, he thought, being late like this.

Hurrying around the corner, Alec ran straight into another roadblock. This one was softer. And noisy. A surprised squeal echoed around him, mingling with the sound of childish cries. In his rush to get to the room, he'd bumped into a dark-haired woman who appeared out of nowhere like a storm, dressed in silver leggings and a bright blue, overly long T-shirt hiked up on one incredibly slender hip.

Weighed down with diaper bag and other paraphernalia, she was holding a squirming baby in her arms.

The howl was deafening. For a split second Alec wasn't sure if the noise was coming from his baby or hers. And then he realized that both were crying, more in startled surprise than anything else.

"Sorry," he apologized, raising his voice to be heard above the din. "I'm in a hurry." Almost automatically, he ran his hand over Andrea's back to soothe her.

Marissa Rogers rubbed her head where it had made stunning contact with his shoulder. The man didn't look particularly muscular, but he obviously had to be. It was either that, or he was smuggling iron rods beneath that green sweater of his.

"That would have been my guess," she replied, amused.

Taking a step back, she felt something tug at chest level. Looking down, she saw that the small pinwheel pin she always wore was stuck to the man's very expensive-looking sweater.

Though he was standing in front of the room, she wondered if he was actually going to attend the session. He didn't look familiar to her and he was certainly dressed all wrong for roughhousing with his baby. That required clothes that were comfortable and worn, not crisp, pressed and stylish.

Her pin threatened to unravel threads out of the carefully crafted sweater if either of them made any sudden moves.

"We seemed to be attached." When he just stared at her, Marissa indicated the pin with her eyes. She shifted

Christopher up higher in her arms, then tried to undo the connection using one hand.

The pin remained firmly entrenched in the sweater. Great, Marissa thought, just what she needed when she was running late. Exasperated, she blew her bangs away from her eyes.

Her baby was squirming, making it impossible to disengage the pin. They were close enough for Alec to take in everything about her and process more information than he normally would. Her eyes were an electric blue that managed to dim the color of the outlandish T-shirt she had on. Her hair was a riot of wisps and curls and yet somehow still looked as if it had been painstakingly arranged that way. Her lips were slightly larger than her oval face and delicate features warranted, keeping her from being beautiful, but definitely not from being engagingly striking.

She was having absolutely no success. "Here, let me try," Alec offered.

He immediately realized his mistake when he reached for the pin. The situation would call for him getting a little more familiar with her than he figured they'd both be comfortable with. He didn't think it would be prudent to be brushing his fingertips along a strange woman's breast, no matter what the reason.

Alec dropped his hand. "Maybe not," he amended. The woman's wide lips pulled into an amused smile and he realized that they didn't keep her from being beautiful. They enhanced her beauty.

"Mammmmaaaamaaa." Christopher was yelling directly into her ear.

Marissa blinked, as if that would help her block out the deafening cry. She raised her eyes to the stranger's. He looked definitely flustered and not happy about it. Marissa attempted to work the pin free again.

"Shh, Mamma's trying to get herself uncoupled from this nice man."

This was ridiculous. Class had probably already started and he was standing out here, being one half of a Siamese twin. "I think you'd do better with two hands," Alec suggested.

"Maybe," she agreed, "but if I put my baby down out here, you'll get to witness a first-class imitation of a gazelle. And I won't be able to do any dashing unless you happen to know how to run backward."

Christopher had been walking ever since he was ten months old and peace as she knew it had gone out the window the moment he had taken his first step. Setting him down here while she was attached to this stranger was just like asking for trouble.

The baby looked as if it was all arms, legs and teeth. It was against Alec's better judgment, but there didn't seem to be much choice.

"Here, let me hold him for you."

Pausing, Marissa looked at the green-eyed stranger. A smile curved her lips again. She nodded at the pink rompered baby in his arms. "You already seem to have your hands full."

Alec shifted Andrea to one arm, holding out his other hand. "I can hold them both."

He fervently hoped he wouldn't wind up embarrassing himself. Together the babies probably weighed only about forty-five pounds or so, but the fact that hers seemed to be in perpetual motion was going to be a definite problem.

Marissa's smile widened. The man looked as if he was getting himself ready for an ordeal. That had to be his first baby, she mused. Still, since no one else appeared to be coming around the bend, letting him hold both children seemed to be the only solution at the moment. And it was getting late.

She presented Christopher to him. "Okay, but you'd better brace yourself." She noted that Chris was setting off the man's daughter, as well.

"Thanks for the warning," **Alec** muttered, accepting the boy, swinging feet and all. Instant contact was made with Alec's stomach. Alec tried not to wince at the unexpected blow.

But Marissa saw it. "Sorry." She flushed ruefully. "I'll hurry."

Very deftly, taking care not to snag the sweater, she worked one of the pinwheel blades loose. Two more to go. How had they managed to tangle themselves up so well so quickly?

She wasn't hurrying fast enough for Christopher, or for the stranger, who was having trouble hanging on to both babies.

"Maaaa-aaaa."

Alec winced, feeling an eardrum shatter. "Good lungs."

The offhand remark evoked a bittersweet pang within Marissa. Stupid, stupid. There was no reason to feel that way. She fumbled with the thread she was trying to ease off the next point of her pin. All that was far behind her now, she reminded herself. More than two years in the past.

"The best." She didn't raise her eyes from what she was doing. "Daddy's a tenor with the Metropolitan Opera." Or was, Marissa amended silently, the last time she'd seen Antonio.

Alec regarded the woman thoughtfully. If her husband was with such a prestigious group, what was she doing out here in leggings and an outlandish shirt, stuck to him? Why wasn't she in New York? Alec glanced at the slender fingers that were fluttering between them, working at the pin.

No ring. Divorced?

Her son made a grab for Alec's ear, obviously determined to destroy by force what he hadn't obliterated with his voice. Alec moved his head back as far as he could. He slanted a glance at the woman. "Could you, um, hurry up with that?"

She almost had it. "One second." Marissa bit her lip ruefully. "I can't believe how tangled it got in just that one collision." The freed thread seemed to bounce back against the sweater. She smoothed it down with her fingertips. "There." She sighed. "We're free." Marissa turned her attention to Christopher, grinning. "I'll take that, thank you."

Alec shifted so that she could easily reclaim her baby. Relief skied over him with the speed of a winter Olympic contender. "All yours."

There was way too much feeling in that proclamation, Marissa thought, amused. At least the man was honest. He made no attempt to pretend that holding on to her wiggling son was a piece of cake. Christopher had worn out a number of baby-sitters in his time. He was the reason she'd opted for this kind of a job while she was trying to earn her masters degree. A degree that had been temporarily interrupted while she took time out to have Christopher and get at least a cursory handle on motherhood. Those hadn't been her original plans, but she had adapted, just as she had adapted when she had discovered that Antonio's plans for the future did not include being a father. With one stroke of a pen, he had shed her, their marriage vows and their unborn child.

Andrea grabbed the collar of Alec's sweater and was hanging on to it as if her very life depended on it. He suspected that sharing space with the woman's bundle of joy might have had something to do with this reaction.

"It's okay, Andrea." He bounced her against his shoulder and she made a noise he swore passed for a giggle. "Daddy's all yours again."

The woman's eyes seemed to glow with warmth as they

washed over his daughter. "Is that her name?" she asked. "Andrea?" Alec nodded, holding the door open for her. "Pretty."

He supposed that some sort of conversation was in order as he followed the woman inside the huge room. Making small talk with strangers had always made him uncomfortable, though he seemed to manage well enough for no one to really notice.

"What's your boy's name?" There was no indication that the child in her arms was a boy. The clothing was neutral, as was the color. And the baby's hair was at a length that could have gone either way. But something told Alec that no female child could yell like that.

"Christopher," Marissa answered.

He'd always liked that name. "Rugged," he commented, looking at the boy. "Suits him."

Marissa cast a long glance around the room. It was filled with brand-new equipment and toys, both purchased and donated, just ripe to set off the imagination. Her classes were happy places that everyone looked forward to attending. And it looked as if everyone was already here. Time to start. "Thanks."

He followed her, wondering if there were assigned places or if people just sat anywhere and milled about. He couldn't have been more out of his element than if he had just tied a bungee cord around his waist.

"Do you know anything about the instructor?" Alec looked around, trying to discern if anyone in the room *looked* like a teacher. "This is my first time here."

So that was it. Marissa turned around to face him. "I didn't think I recognized you." She tried to remember if there was a new name on the register. People came and went so frequently, it was hard to keep track. The classes were relatively unstructured, which was what attracted most parents to them. It was a place to exhale, to be shown that they hadn't terminally ruined their offspring by misguided deeds, and to feel good about parenting, themselves and their children.

Judging by the turnout, she figured she was doing a good job of reaching her goals.

Andrea was wetting his sweater just below the snag, trying to suck it all into her mouth. Alec moved her to his other side. "I just registered."

Marissa nodded at several mothers looking her way, then smiled brightly at the man. "Well, then, welcome to the class. I'm Marissa Rogers."

Alec was feeling increasingly more uncomfortable. By his rapid count, there were only three other men here. He began to wonder if this had been such a good idea after all.

"Looks like the teacher's one of those people who doesn't take responsibility seriously."

"Oh?" She arched a sharp brow in response to his observation. "What makes you say that?"

He shrugged, looking toward the door. "Well, she's obviously later than we are."

The smile on her lips was vaguely amused. "Not quite."

Before he could ask her what she meant by that, she'd hurried away from him.

Alec watched her work her way up to the front of the room, shedding her diaper bag and her purse as she went. Judging by the way everyone greeted her, she was no stranger to the group. Holding Andrea against him, he moved in the woman's wake, deciding that he might do better staying near someone who was aware of the routine.

Alec stopped dead and realized his mistake as soon as the woman turned around and addressed the people in the room.

"Sorry I'm late, everybody. Why don't we all get started?"

There was a reason why she looked as if she knew the
routine. She made up the routine.

"Score one for Daddy, Andrea," Alec muttered under
his breath.

Coming to terms with the fact that he hadn't exactly put
his best foot forward, Alec moved over to one side of the
room. With luck, maybe he could blend into the crowd.

Once she'd gotten the session started and had broken up
parents and children into small play groups, Marissa walked
around the room, observing and giving advice or helpful
hints wherever needed. She knew the value of a well-placed
suggestion, an encouraging word. Out of the corner of her
eye, she watched the newcomer. She knew she'd never seen
him before. There was no way a man like that could blend
into the crowd and be forgotten. He had a take-charge manner about him, even when being intimidated by a roomful
of one-year-olds.

He really did seem to love his little girl, she thought.
He'd have to, to be going through something like this with
her. The man looked as if he felt like a fish out of water.

"That's very good, Mrs. Berg." She patted the woman's
shoulder. "Just remember to guide Shelly's hand through
the exercise."

Widening her smile and adding to her directions the
touch of warmth that she prided herself on, Marissa made
her way over to Alec's side of the room.

He was on the floor, his legs spread out wide in front of
him, with Andrea propped up against him. There was no
one else around them.

Marissa squatted to his level. "You're not doing anything."

She'd surprised him. Alec cleared his throat, wishing he
didn't feel like such a damn fool.

"Yes, I am. We're sitting here, watching everyone else."

He shrugged, feeling himself get defensive. "She seems content." He caught hold of the edge of Andrea's shirt just as she was beginning to crawl off and prove him a liar.

"Oh, but it's no fun to just watch, is it, sweetheart?" Marissa scooped up the little girl. Chris was safely ensconced and busy interacting with a gaggle of other children and their parents. It was an unspoken rule that everyone in class helped look out for the little boy while Marissa worked. No one really seemed to mind. If anything, it was combat training under fire.

Holding Andrea, she looked down at Alec. "She's supposed to burn up some of that pent-up baby energy when she's here." Marissa couldn't help smiling as she looked the man over. "Looks to me as if she's worn you out."

Alec gained his feet, dusting off the back of his pants. "She does her best." He was here to take advantage of what the program had to offer, there was no reason to feel awkward with the instructor. He took the plunge. "All right, what do you suggest?"

Still holding Andrea, she turned toward the bright yellow, blue and red interwove mesh that stood off to the side of the room. People were lined up to take their turn with their babies.

"How about the jungle gym? Lots of opportunity for her to stretch that little body."

Alec looked at the netting dubiously. "And to break it."

Oh, a worrier. She would have never pegged him for one of those. Marissa found it rather sweet.

"You'd be surprised at how resilient these little creatures are. C'mon," she offered, "I'll show you." Then, not waiting for him, she began to walk toward the jungle gym.

"All right, I suppose we're both game. And seeing as how you've got my daughter, I guess I have no choice."

She glanced at him over her shoulder. "Oh, no, Mr.—

Beckett is it?'' Alec nodded. ''You always have a choice, no matter what.''

She sounded as if she meant that, he thought. Fiercely.

Standing back and letting her work, Alec watched with interest as Marissa put his limber little baby through a series of paces that had the little girl laughing with glee. The laugh was infectious, striking down both babies and parents alike. Alec felt himself grinning.

She had such a natural aptitude with children, he thought. And she certainly seemed to like being around them.

Slowly an idea, more like a prayer really, began to take form in his mind.

Maybe it was crazy, but he'd never know until he asked. Alec began silently rehearsing his offer and waiting for an opportunity to open up.

Chapter Two

For a moment Alec considered leaving Andrea at the jungle gym. No less than three mothers had volunteered to look after her along with their own offspring. But in the end, he opted to tuck his daughter onto his hip as he went to corner the agile instructor. He wasn't all that keen on leaving his daughter with strangers, even nice ones.

Marissa was all the way at the other end of the large room. By the time he had made it over to her, he'd had to change direction three times and felt as if he was trying to catch a butterfly. The toddlers in the class weren't the only ones with an endless supply of energy.

"Excuse me. Excuse me." Weaving his way around the last obstacle—a woman with an exuberant twin firmly tethered to each hand—Alec finally managed to get close enough to Marissa to call out to her. "Mrs. Rogers, could I speak to you?"

Her arms full of wiggling child, Marissa turned around. He looked harried, she thought, an amused smile tugging at her mouth. It warmed her heart every time she saw a man taking the trouble to play his role as a father to the fullest. It proved to her that there were good fathers out there, even if neither her father nor Antonio had managed to take on the role with any grace or flare.

"Sure, if you call me Marissa. When you call me Mrs. Rogers, I have this urge to look over my shoulder to see if my mother is standing there."

With an approving nod, she handed the little boy she was holding to the child's mother. No sooner were her arms free than Andrea made a grab for her. Without missing a beat, Marissa took the little girl into her arms.

He was amazed at how easily Andrea seemed to take to the woman. It just reinforced his feelings about his decision.

"Then you're not married?" The question came out of nowhere, nudging aside the one he thought he was going to ask.

She laughed softly, shaking her head. Though she considered herself to be a warm, friendly person, there were certain personal things she was reluctant to share. And what had happened between her and Antonio came under that heading.

Brushing Andrea's wispy blond hair back from her face, Marissa evaded the question. "Not to my father, no." Whenever she mentioned or thought of the Sergeant, it always evoked the same image for her. An open suitcase. It seemed as if she'd spent her entire childhood either packing or unpacking one, traipsing around the country because her father had signed his life away to the army.

Andrea seemed bent on restructuring Marissa's face. Taking the little hand in hers to keep Andrea from widening her mouth, Marissa pressed a kiss to the busy fingers. Andrea cooed. Raising her eyes to Alec's gaze, Marissa waited for him to continue. "Is that what you wanted to ask me?"

She knew it wasn't. This wasn't the kind of place a man

came to meet women. Even if it was, he didn't look like the type. Alec Beckett gave every impression that he was very Ivy League, very businesslike. Even in supposedly casual clothes, he looked ready to leap into a board meeting at a moment's notice. She wondered what he did for a living and if he ever loosened up.

Alec noticed that Marissa didn't seem to be distracted by the fact that Andrea was trying to climb up her body. If anything, she appeared to be at ease, as if it was all natural. An admiration for a talent he knew was way beyond him took hold.

"No, um…" Alec surveyed the crowded room. "Could we talk?"

Deftly, Marissa pried childish fingers away from her gold chain, a gift from her brothers and sisters when she graduated high school. It was her one cherished possession.

"Isn't that what we're doing now, Mr. Beckett?"

Marissa glanced toward the play area to see how Christopher was doing. Cyndee, a three-month veteran of the class and her self-appointed assistant, was watching over him as well as her own daughter and another child. The hopelessly perky woman was braver than most people here, Marissa mused. Everything seemed to be under control.

"I mean privately." Alec wasn't prepared to discuss business with an audience around.

He sounded serious. Marissa wondered if something was bothering him. He wouldn't be the first parent who had sought her out for a sympathetic ear.

The room was full of parents and babies. It seemed as if each class was larger than the last. Not that she minded; she took it as a compliment. Marissa nodded over to the side.

"I'm afraid that a corner is the best I can do under the circumstances. Unless you want to wait until after class."

"A corner will do fine." He wanted her to have some

time to think about what he had to propose. If he waited until after class, she might be too tired and automatically turn him down. He didn't want to be turned down.

Alec followed Marissa. He noticed that several of the mothers were looking at him knowingly, as if the word "novice" were still stamped on his forehead. Sometimes, he had to admit, he felt that way. One year and he was still feeling his way around this maze called fatherhood.

Marissa leaned against the beige wall and looked up at him, waiting.

She had to have the bluest eyes he'd ever seen. So blue that they could have easily made him lose his train of thought. Because he suddenly felt awkward, Alec took his daughter from her. Holding Andrea gave him something to do, somewhere else to look besides her eyes.

Whenever he made presentations, he always strove for a good opening line. He knew the value of capturing his audience's attention right from the start. But none occurred to him now. Making the best of it, Alec plunged in, stumbling.

"I noticed how good you are with the children."

Marissa smiled. Where was he going with this? "The job kind of calls for it." She saw at least three mothers who required her attention. She hoped that whatever Beckett had to say, he'd get to it quickly.

"I was wondering if you're that good on a one-to-one basis." This wasn't going well, he thought.

Marissa turned her head back toward him with a jerk. He had her full attention now. She stared at him, voicing her thoughts aloud.

"Are you *hitting* on me?" Maybe she hadn't gotten to be a good judge of character after all.

Completely wrapped up in the dilemma he found himself in, Alec took a moment to fully process her question.

"What?" Talk about wrong impressions. She thought he

was trying to pick her up, he realized. Belatedly, he remembered he'd asked her if she was married. What else was she supposed to think? "Oh, no, really." He'd denied it so adamantly, he knew that he inadvertently was sending out the wrong message. "I mean, not that you're not pretty, you are. Very. Maybe even beautiful, but—" He stopped abruptly before he managed to make a complete fool of himself. He was hanging by a thread now. Alec's laugh was rueful. "I'm not saying this very well, am I?"

He had a nice smile, she thought. Not merely a pleasant one, a really nice one. A smile that spoke of sincerity and went straight to the soul. Taking pity on him, she gently eased him off the hook.

"Well, the words pretty and beautiful can't be held against you, but, no, you're not." She saw a woman waving at her to catch her attention. "I'm afraid I have to hurry you along, Mr. Beckett. What is your point?"

Alec felt disgusted with himself. How the hell could a man who could conduct meetings involving several hundred people be so tongue-tied when it came to talking to just one petite woman?

Because he wasn't in his element, he reminded himself. His element contained software programs, computers. Sterile things, not things that required a sterilized environment. He glanced down at Andrea who was once again attempting to see just how much of his sweater she could stuff into her mouth. With an inward sigh, Alec eased the expensive wool out past tiny pink lips.

Marissa was beginning to edge away. If he didn't talk quickly, he knew he was going to lose her. "My nanny quit."

She couldn't help herself. The declaration begged for a comeback. "Aren't you a little old for a nanny, Mr. Beckett?"

For a second he thought she was serious. The amusement

in her eyes set him straight. Humor. He realized that in the past year he'd almost forgotten how to laugh.

"No, I mean, Andrea's. Andrea's nanny quit."

She stood on her toes, as if that would make her voice carry better. "I'll be right there, Mrs. Stewart," she promised the woman who was waving at her. Marissa turned back to Beckett, laying a hand on his arm. The moment instantly turned private.

"I know." Marissa laughed. "Forgive me, but you looked as if you needed to be teased a little. I'm sorry, it was a poor joke. You were saying?"

Her eyes were so brilliant, so animated, they reminded him of the lake outside his window when the sun reflected on the calm water. It took him a second to retrieve his thoughts from their grasp.

Andrea, frustrated that she couldn't teeth on her father's sweater, squealed. "Andrea's nanny quit last night and I was wondering if—"

Marissa nodded, finishing his thought. "I know of anyone for the job?"

She was only half right. "Actually, I was thinking more along the lines of you for the job."

Marissa blinked. Had she missed something? Why would Beckett think that she needed a job? In light of what was presently going on in her life, the suggestion was particularly stunning.

"Me?"

She looked dumbstruck. Oh, God, he hoped he hadn't insulted her somehow. But he was desperate and desperate men did desperate things. Alec began talking quickly. "Yes, you'd be perfect. The kids all seem to respond to you."

He'd already said that, she thought. Marissa began moving toward Mrs. Stewart again. She did have a job to do and she wasn't seeing to it by standing here, talking to him.

"Well, I thank you for the compliment, but as you can see, I already have a job. One that I really should be doing."

He wasn't giving up that easily. Not after seeing the way Andrea took to her. Andrea had always cried whenever a new nanny came into her life.

"Is this full-time? Your job?" God, just listen to him. He was talking as if English were his second language.

Teaching the classes was only a part-time job. Luckily, she did have Antonio's child support checks. Though he had loudly proclaimed himself not to be father material, that much he had been willing to give of himself. The checks, the scholarship money the university had awarded her and an incredible ability to live on a shoestring was all she really needed.

Marissa saw no reason to go into any of that with Beckett. "No, but my time is pretty well taken up."

"With Christopher?" It didn't take a genius to guess that.

Her smile was so wide it dominated her face and slipped up into her eyes. "Yes."

Alec pounced. He'd been prepared for that objection when he'd made his offer. "You could bring him with you. What I really need is a live-in nanny." It would make things a lot easier, but he could be flexible. Desperate men were. "But since you're married, I could—"

Maybe she should clear that up, she decided. There was no reason to have Beckett laboring under a misconception.

"I'm not married. Anymore," she added. "But that's not the problem, Mr. Beckett. I go to school three nights and one day a week."

He only heard what he needed to hear. "You're not married?"

He wasn't getting the message. "No," Marissa said firmly. "But—"

Alec's mind moved faster than her protest. "Then you could be a live-in."

"If I needed to be, but—"

Relief was a heady thing and he let it wash over him. He hadn't expected to get this lucky. Thank God he'd opted to register for this class.

"This is great. I work at home two to three days a week." It was part of Bytes and Pieces' policy to help solve Southern California's escalating gridlock problem rather than add to it. All that had been needed was a terminal connected to the main computer at the office and he was on his way. "Something could be worked out."

Temporarily forgetting about Mrs. Stewart, Marissa addressed the more pressing problem: getting through Beckett's thick head. She raised her voice. "Yes, if I wanted it to, but, Mr. Beckett, you're missing a crucial point here."

He ceased mentally patting himself on the back. "I am?"

"Yes." She looked up at him, carefully enunciating each word. "I said no."

The foundation of the Arch of Triumph he was constructing suffered a terminal crack. He tried to smooth it over.

"Not in so many words," Alec observed quickly.

The man had to be a salesman. "Actually, in a lot of words, some of which you wouldn't allow me to get out. I have a very full schedule and I really don't need to take on any more right now."

He had a feeling about Marissa and Andrea. She would be good for his daughter. He wasn't about to give up without a fight. "How much are they paying you here?"

His question caught her off guard. "That's a little personal, don't you think?"

Alec shook his head. He wasn't trying to pry, he was trying to win. "Money is never personal. It's a very public thing. Whatever it is, I can double it."

The man didn't know how to take no for an answer. Given his looks and the expensive cut of his clothing, she suspected that he probably didn't hear it very often. "I take it that you're used to getting what you want?"

He realized that honesty carried weight with her. It was gut feeling, but he went with it.

"No, just not used to being this desperate. I've had four nannies for Andrea in a year. Four women I hand-picked after long, exhausting sessions of talking to enough women to easily fill up a convention hall. They all came from reputable agencies and had long, glowing references in their possession, but things just didn't work out."

She wondered if the women left because of some problem that had to do with him. She couldn't see how it could have been because of Andrea. "Why is that?"

He thought for a moment, trying to remember. "Ellen left because she fell in love with someone who was leaving town. Celeste decided that she wasn't cut out to be a nanny. I fired Sue. Ingrid, the first nanny, retired. I think Andrea might have had something to do with that. There's no getting away from the fact that she's a handful." He thought of Christopher. Andrea was positively docile in comparison. "But I think you're used to that."

Marissa couldn't help smiling. Christopher was a live wire by anyone's definition. "You might say that."

Good, he had her attention. Alec didn't let the opportunity slip away. "Anyway, I really don't have the time to go through the process again. I'm in the middle of marketing this new software I developed and the thought of sitting and listening to the peccadilloes of a squadron of women while I try to separate fact from fiction to find a woman who has enough love, patience and enthusiasm to handle my daughter is particularly daunting right now." He gave it his best shot. "Especially when I've found a woman who would be perfect for the job."

Marissa sighed. He was giving her an awful lot of credit. Either that, or he really was serious about dreading the thought of conducting interviews. Either way, she couldn't help him.

"Well, I thank you for that, but speaking of jobs…" She glanced over her shoulder at the group. Mrs. Stewart had been inordinately patient. She had to answer the woman's question and start the new game portion of the class. "I should be getting back to mine."

He had thought that he was winning her over. "What about my offer?"

"It's a very flattering one, but I'm afraid I'm going to have to pass." She was walking backward, away from him, and managed, somehow, to avoid colliding with anyone or stepping on any of the toddlers that were almost everywhere he looked. The woman was uncanny. "But I'll let you know if I find someone who can live up to your specifications."

"Outside of Mother Teresa, Mary Poppins and you," he murmured to himself, "I don't know of anyone." Temporarily deflated, Alec looked at his daughter. He had to be in the office tomorrow. This wasn't going to go over well with his mother. "Do you think your grandmother is up to taking you for another day?"

Andrea screwed up her face and made a familiar sound. Alec looked around for someplace where he could change his daughter. There was a change table against the far wall and he headed toward it just as Marissa called for attention.

"Don't tell Roberta I called her that," he whispered to Andrea. "Or she'll really walk out on us."

Andrea grunted again. Alec walked faster.

Roberta Beckett smoothed back her carefully styled auburn hair with a perfectly manicured hand. Two-inch-long fingernails flickered in the air like mauve butterflies searching for a place to alight. Through a meticulous regime that she adhered to religiously, Roberta managed to look years younger than the age written on the birth certificate tucked away in her safe-deposit box. Alec knew it was one of her greatest sources of pride that most people, upon seeing her with him, mistook them for brother and sister.

"It's not that I don't love her, Alec. I do. I truly do." Roberta spared a smile for the child, who was holding on to the webbed siding of the portable crib and bouncing up and down in place. "But this rocking, feeding, diapering..." Her deep, husky voice dropped an octave lower as she said the last distasteful word. "It just isn't me."

Who knew that better than he? Still, his back was against the wall; he wouldn't have asked her any other way. Besides, he knew for a fact that the housekeeper performed the actual dirty work. All Roberta did was add her stamp of approval.

"I know, Roberta, and I appreciate you putting yourself out like this, but—"

She didn't want his gratitude, she wanted results. "Haven't you found anyone yet?"

He hadn't even had time to call the agency. He supposed he should have begun interviews yesterday instead of going to class with Andrea, but when he'd signed up, he hadn't planned on the nanny quitting.

Mentally, he took inventory to make sure he'd brought everything that Dorothy, his mother's housekeeper, would need to take care of Andrea. "Ellen only quit a little more than twenty-four hours ago."

The argument obviously carried no weight with Roberta. "God created the world in six days."

His mother had her own brand of logic. He had ceased to try to make sense of it a long time ago. "He left Adam and Eve for last. That was the hardest part."

Roberta sniffed. Andrea squealed with glee, then landed

on a well-padded bottom and a stuffed rabbit. "You don't have to create a nanny, just hire one."

He had to get going. Rex, one of the two owners of the company, was his best friend and incredibly understanding, but there were limits. "Almost as difficult."

Roberta gave him a reproving look. "I never had difficulties finding one for you."

Alec thought of the women who had paraded through his life, the ones who had been there to substitute for the genuine article. The very memory was enough to make him not want to hire anyone. He'd had a disjointed, unstable childhood at best. He hadn't wanted that for Andrea. But he obviously had no choice. Alec sincerely hoped she wouldn't remember any of this.

Because he needed help, he threw the ball into Roberta's court. "All right, then you do it. You find a nanny."

"Me? I should think that would be something you would want to handle on your own." Roberta pursed her lips in a disapproving pout. "Really, Alec, I thought I raised you more independently than that."

She was unorthodox, but he loved her. That still didn't make him incline to let her delude herself.

"No, Roberta, you didn't raise me at all. Estelle and Elizabeth and Suzanne and Joan and several other women whose names and faces begin to escape me, they raised me."

She distanced herself the way she always did when faced with something she didn't want to deal with. A frown brought with it several wrinkles that refused to be smoothed, creamed or coaxed away. "What is your point?"

There was a vague discomfort in her eyes. Any moment now she'd announce that she was going off on a junket somewhere, leaving him completely adrift. He had to do something before that happened.

Alec looked at his mother ruefully. "The point is that

I'm a little stressed out right now and I guess I'm being rude.''

Roberta smiled, graciously accepting the apology. ''Yes, you are. But I forgive you because, after all, I am your mother even if I don't look it.''

She walked Alec to the front door. ''I'll watch her today but remember, this can't go on forever. I want you to find a nanny quickly.''

''No more than me, Roberta,'' he assured her. ''No more than me.''

''By tomorrow,'' she called after him.

With any luck, tomorrow could be one of the days he worked out of the office he had set up in his den. That would give him the opportunity to conduct a few interviews. If conducting interviews for a nanny could be referred to as an opportunity.

He fervently hoped it would be the last time he'd have to go through this.

''Thanks, Jane, you're a lifesaver.'' Marissa shed her sweater, draping it over the back of the kitchen chair. Class had run over. Professor Johnston had gotten into a heated discussion with one of the students over the administration of corporal punishment and the class, divided, had taken sides. She was more than half an hour late. She'd called Jane from the campus, but that hadn't changed the fact that it was way past the time she'd promised to be back.

Jane gathered her books together, depositing them into her backpack. She grinned. ''Hey, no problem. Think of it as payback time. I remember when you used to baby-sit me.'' The young girl got up. ''You made things so much fun.''

The Sergeant had been stationed here for a while when Marissa was in her mid-teens. She'd always liked baby-sitting at the Hendersons. Their house always seemed to be so comfortably disorganized. Not the pristine living quarters that the Sergeant insisted on. "I liked you, it was easy."

Jane nodded over her shoulder toward the tiny alcove off the living room. "Christopher is in bed."

"Asleep?"

It was a rhetorical question. If he hadn't been, Marissa knew she would have heard him by now. He wasn't a child who didn't make himself known.

Jane nodded. "I think we tired each other out."

She'd already called her father and knew he was on his way to pick her up. He'd be out front by the time she got down to the ground level.

Jane was at the door when she suddenly remembered. "Oh, and you had a phone call. I took the number down. It's posted on the refrigerator."

"Thanks." Marissa handed Jane her money. "And good night."

"Same time Thursday?"

"You bet." Marissa locked the door and crossed to the refrigerator. Taking the paper from under the magnet, she stared it at. The number wasn't familiar.

But the name was. Jeremy Allen. The man she was subletting the apartment from. Tucking the phone number into her jeans, she first crossed to the alcove to check on Christopher.

He was still asleep. She stood, looking at him, love swelling within her heart. During the day Christopher was sheer energy, but once he was down, he was down for the night. It was, she supposed, nature's little way of compensating.

She was still smiling to herself as she dialed the phone number. A sleepy voice answered on the fourth ring and said what passed for hello.

"Jeremy? This is Marissa." She glanced at the clock and

realized what time it was in New York. She'd completely forgotten about the time difference. "Oh, God, did I wake you?"

"Yeah, but that's okay." She heard rustling on the other end, as if he was sitting up in bed. "I've got some news."

Marissa didn't know if she particularly liked the sound of that. It was the exact same way her father used to preface his announcements that they were moving yet again.

"Oh?"

"Yeah, I'm coming home."

She could feel her stomach sinking down to the floor. The apartment was a godsend for her. Located just a couple of miles from the campus and close to both her job and Jane, it made her life easy.

Easy was obviously not a word destined to remain with any permanence in her life. "When?"

"End of the week."

"The end of the week?" When she'd agreed to sublet the apartment, Jeremy had said that he was leaving for two years. It had only been nine months. "But you said—"

It was clear that he didn't feel up to being hassled when he was half asleep. "That this was only temporary," he reminded her.

She could barely afford to live here. How was she going to pay for a regular apartment and still go to school? "Yes, but you made it sound as if it was until the end of next year—at the very least."

He didn't sound any happier than she did about the need to return home. "It was, but the funding for the play ran out. We closed today." Jeremy let out a long sigh. "I could let you stay on. Of course, it'd be a little tight."

In more ways than one, she thought. It was all right to deal with Jeremy when he was three thousand miles away. But she knew what close proximity would bring and she wasn't up to the struggle involved with keeping him at arm's length all the time. Jeremy believed that no woman should die without experiencing the pleasure of having slept with him, at least once.

"That's all right," she told him. "I'll be out by the end of the week." Oh, God.

"You're sure?"

"I'm sure." He yawned in her ear. "You'd better get some sleep," she urged. "I'll see you Friday."

"Let me know if you change your mind. I'm a big-hearted guy."

"Right." Marissa hung up, frowning. She had four days to find a place to live, work on her thesis, study for an exam and juggle all the other various parts of her life.

Marissa felt as if she'd just hit the legendary wall. And it had fallen on top of her.

Chapter Three

Marissa hurried into the room, just barely making it in time. The clock on the back wall announced that it was exactly five-thirty.

Made it.

She was only vaguely aware that Christopher had his fingers tangled in the ends of her hair and was apparently intent on seeing how resilient it was. The tugging on her scalp registered peripherally and she moved his hand away. Undaunted, he went to work on the neck of her T-shirt.

A quick scan of the room told her that everyone seemed to be here. She had made class by the skin of her teeth. Again. This had to stop. Up until last month, she'd always been so organized.

Like a drill sergeant.

She supposed, in a way, she wasn't all that different from her father. Marissa raised her brow. Now there was a frightening thought. She wasn't anything like the Sergeant, she was just feeling slightly punchy, that's all.

Concerned about having to look for a new place to live,

she'd tossed and turned all night. And when she'd finally dropped off, Christopher had woken up, loudly announcing the beginning of a brand new day. A day that had three classes and a trip to the library crammed into it. The latter had turned into nothing short of a disaster. Every book she needed for her thesis had been checked out. There hadn't been time to try another library.

Lately there didn't seem to be enough time to do anything except rush.

The classified section she'd grabbed this morning on her way out the door was no closer to being read now than it had been when she'd left the apartment at eight. It had spent the day sticking up out of her purse, a constant reminder that she hadn't had the time to look through it yet.

She was a little afraid of opening it. Afraid to see just what apartments within the area were going for now. Undoubtedly it had to be a lot more than she was able to wring out of her already-squeezed-to-the-limit budget. There was no way that she was going to be able to afford an apartment on her own. Though she hated the idea, she was going to have to find a roommate.

With her master's thesis weighing heavily on her mind, the prospect of looking for an apartment *and* a roommate was almost more than Marissa could handle. She could feel it wearing away at her, eroding her optimism like a steady drip eventually erodes the surface of a rock.

It was beginning to seem, Marissa thought, as if life just never got easier.

Heads turned in her direction as the door behind her closed with a resounding slam. She hadn't meant to let go of it. Marissa flashed a smile at those closest to her. Reaching over to set her purse on the floor, she accidentally dropped the folded newspaper. She felt disjointed and uncoordinated.

Marissa sighed, gathering her patience together. She was

going to get through this, just as she had managed to get through every other bumpy segment of her life. If she'd gotten some sleep, she wouldn't feel this frazzled.

Still, sometimes it would be nice just to have one thing to handle at a time. Like getting her thesis completed.

Securing Christopher on her hip, Marissa bent to pick up the scattered pages. She was definitely going to go through them right after class. Just before she collapsed into a boneless heap.

"Let me get that for you."

Marissa glanced up to see that the offer had come from Beckett. She bit back the impulse to say that she could manage. Right now, she couldn't.

"That would be very nice," she murmured, straightening again.

With one eye on Andrea who was on the floor, communing with two other babies, Alec squatted and quickly gathered up the paper.

Marissa dragged her free hand through her hair. The damp air had made it curl like a plateful of curly fries. It felt hopelessly tangled. A little, she mused, like her life right now.

"Thanks." She took the paper from him, then smiled ruefully. "I seem to be coming apart today."

Not that he'd noticed. Alec allowed his eyes to wander up and down her frame. She was wearing hot pink leggings and a pristine white top today. He wondered how long it would remain that way, given that her son was tugging a piece of it toward his mouth.

He smiled at her. "Then you must have gotten your hands on one hell of an adhesive because all your parts seem to be holding together damn well from what I can see."

He was flirting with her, she thought. The effect was not unpleasant. In the midst of the classroom, it was harmless enough and God knew it felt good to hear when she was feeling like an A-1 ugly duckling with frizzy hair.

"Thanks." The dimple at the corner of her mouth winked as she grinned. "I needed that more than having the papers picked up."

She has a nice smile, Alec thought. Hell, she has a nice everything. If he were in the market for that sort of thing, he added silently. Which he wasn't.

The only thing he was in the market for right now was a nanny. Fast. Just the thought of the pending interviews lined up for him tomorrow made him uneasy. He glanced at Marissa, wondering if asking her one more time might make her reconsider his offer.

He never got the chance to find out.

Setting the classifieds out of the way, Marissa turned her attention to the rest of the class. If she didn't get started, there was no way the class would end on time. She didn't believe in shortchanging people just because she was having personal problems.

Alec picked Andrea up from the floor and found a spot in the front of the room. "Time to get you limber, Andy," he whispered against the downy softness of her cornsilk hair. He took her gurgle to be agreement.

Individual chatter died away quickly. The only sound that remained was that of babies cooing and fussing.

Marissa smiled ruefully at the people in the first few rows. "Well, I see that I'm the last one here again. I'm really sorry," she apologized with feeling, "but I seem to be running behind lately."

A sympathetic, commiserating murmur rippled through the group. Everyone, it seemed, had been there, or was still there. Babies had a habit of upending lives.

Marissa found looking out on the sea of familiar faces comforting. It helped nudge her problems into the background. At least temporarily. These people weren't paying good money to come to class just to see a woman nearing the end of her rope. They were here for guidance, bless 'em. And to be shown creative games they could play with their children, games that were geared toward teaching as well as fun.

Most of all, they were here because they loved their children. It gave them all a common bond. A special bond. No one knew better than she did the importance of parental love. Or how it felt to grow up without it.

She looked around the room slowly, making eye contact with as many people as she could. "All right, people, let's get started, shall we?"

She was preoccupied, he would make book on it.

Alec was well acquainted with the signs. They'd been there, in his own mirror, countless times over the past year. Today had been no exception.

The look that was in her eyes had stared back at him this morning while he was shaving. Preoccupied, he'd almost managed to slice his face. He'd been worrying about finding if not the perfect nanny, at least a tolerable one, preferably with stamina.

Alec couldn't help wondering what Marissa's dilemma concerned and if there was any way that they could wind up helping each other. If he did something for her, then maybe she would agree to...

He was really beginning to think like a desperate man, he upbraided himself.

"How could a man feel desperate, having someone like you in his life?" he asked Andrea. She ignored him, trying to swallow her foot whole. Laughing, Alec redirected her attention to the business at hand.

Out of the corner of his eye he watched Marissa as she wandered from parent to parent, giving advice, encouragement and always, tacit approval. Her genuine enthusiasm was infectious. Everyone, he noted, vied for her attention. They were all seated on the floor, most with their offspring planted between their legs, struggling to put the toddlers through the paces of the new exercise she had just introduced.

Marissa was determined to get to everyone at least once during the session. She stopped by one mother whose baby, howling in protest, was trying to make a break for freedom. Each time the woman let go of him, he would start crawling away.

It looked amusing, but Marissa knew how frustrating it could be. "Try this," she suggested. Using the little boy as a model, Marissa demonstrated how to stretch the young muscles without placing undue pressure on them. The boy stopped squirming.

Success. Marissa rose, nodding at the boy's mother. "Now you."

Hesitantly, the woman mimicked what she had been shown. Marissa's grin was wide as she squeezed her shoulder. "That's it. Have fun with it." She began picking her way around the room again. "That's why you're here," she told the others, "to have fun with your baby."

Another woman waved to get Marissa's attention. "Is this right?"

"As long as neither you nor your baby turn into a pretzel, it's right." Marissa watched as the woman demonstrated her own interpretation of the stretching exercise, then nodded. "Remember, creativity is the key. Be flexible. Inventive. This isn't so much about form as it is about making sure your baby gets a healthy dose of exercise."

"How much is enough?" someone asked.

"As much as either one of you can take. You'll know when it happens," she promised. Marissa stopped to ruffle one baby's amazing mop of black hair. The baby gurgled in response. "These babies have energy, use it positively.

For you, not against you. Tire them out naturally, instead of having them become comatose in front of a TV set."

Alec looked up, surprised. "You don't like television?"

Marissa turned in the direction of the question. Beckett. She couldn't picture him planting his daughter in front of a television set. He seemed too attentive to the little girl's needs.

"Oh, I love TV, but just not as a perpetual baby-sitter."

That had been her mother's solution and she had taken to it wholeheartedly. So much so that as Marissa was growing up in her nomadic existence, at times it seemed as if the TV was her only friend. It had taken willpower and determination for her to break the habit and stop hiding in a make-believe world. She'd made certain that her siblings didn't make her mistake.

"Too many parents plant their kids in front of a TV set and leave them there. Then they're surprised five years later to find out that their son or daughter has turned into a couch potato with no interest in getting any exercise."

Just as Marissa began to kneel, Andrea scooted through her legs. Marissa grabbed the edge of the little girl's smock in time to prevent her from colliding with another baby. She stilled Andrea's squeal of protest with a hug.

She was quick, Alec thought as he reclaimed his daughter from Marissa's arms. Andrea was developing a nasty habit of wanting to go off exploring on her own. He knew he should encourage it, but he worried about her getting hurt. Maybe he was being too cautious. He wished there was someone to turn to to help him over the rough spots.

"I don't think there's any danger of either one of you becoming couch potatoes," he commented. Not with moves like that.

Marissa inclined her head, acknowledging his assessment. She thought of the pace her life had taken on lately.

A sigh escaped before she could prevent it. She saw the curious look in Beckett's eyes.

"I think I might like that, actually. Kicking back and sitting on a sofa—one that didn't have work piled up all over it."

He would have bet that there wasn't anything about her that was disorganized. Maybe he was wrong. "Are you talking about laundry or a business you run out of the house?"

"Neither." Marissa thought of the state she had left her living room in this morning. Her sofa was littered with pads of notes that had to do with her thesis. The thesis that would determine whether or not she was going to graduate. "I'm talking about schoolbooks."

He had a feeling that she didn't just exclusively teach Baby and Me classes. "Then you're a real teacher? I mean, you teach someplace else?"

"No, I learn someplace else." She'd already told him that she was going to school, there was no harm in elaborating. "I'm going for my master's degree. Child psychology," she continued. Marissa looked toward her son. Having used him in her original demonstration, she had left Christopher in Cyndee's care as she made her way around the room. "I want to know what makes them tick as well as how their bodies work."

He didn't begin to fool himself into believing that he would *ever* understand how his daughter's mind worked. She was only a year old and he was already having trouble second-guessing her reactions. It would only get harder as time went on. "Sounds like a lifetime study."

She laughed, thinking of the theory she was developing in her thesis. "Tell me about it."

Impulse took over, putting words into his mouth before they were fully formed in his head. "I'd like to. Over coffee.'' Alec looked at Marissa hopefully. ''Maybe after class?''

She was tempted. But then she squelched the reaction. It wasn't a good idea. The last thing she wanted was to see one of her male students socially. Her life was complicated enough as it was.

''I don't think—''

''Strictly student and teacher.'' He clarified his invitation so quickly that she was embarrassed for thinking that he'd meant socially. ''I've got some questions I need to ask you and you're a hard lady to corner for more than a couple of minutes at a time.''

''Marissa,'' a woman called to her.

Alec grinned, his point validated. ''See what I mean?''

Her mouth curved as she nodded. ''Yes.''

''Is that yes, you see what I mean, or yes, you'll go out with me for coffee?''

She answered before she let herself think about it. If she stopped to think, she would have been forced to refuse. She had too much else to do. Time was ticking away.

''Both.''

''Great.'' A pleased feeling spread through Alec that seemed somewhat disproportionate to what had transpired. But then Andrea tried to make another break for it and Alec found his attention drawn elsewhere.

Alec would have never thought of Squirrely Joe's as a place to take a woman for a cup of coffee. For one thing, the cups were made out of cardboard. For another, so was their coffee. The Squirrely Joe's located two miles from where the Baby and Me classes were held was part of a fast-food chain that served up remarkably appetizing junk food. Making a proper cup of coffee was very low on their priority list, right after degreasing the overhead oven fans.

But Squirrely Joe's was where Marissa said she wanted to go when he asked her. So, Squirrely Joe's it was.

With both babies safely nestled in their respective portable car seats, Alec and Marissa carried them into the restaurant. The interior was decorated like a cartoon forest. An overhead speaker piped in appropriate sounds. Alec supposed the place was not without its charm, if you were crazy about cartoons.

Sliding the infant seats into the booth first, they sat down on opposites sides of the table. Alec waited a moment to see if Andrea would wake up. But she went on sleeping.

He rose, taking out his wallet. Marissa was reaching for her purse.

"I asked you out, the least I can do is spring for it." Coffee came in small and large. Medium didn't seem to be an option. Even the large didn't amount to more than a dollar. He was accustomed to spending more. Alec nodded at the highlighted menu behind the counter. "Are you sure you only want coffee?"

Marissa turned in her seat and found herself looking up at an artistically enhanced poster of a foaming strawberry malt that hung between the breakfast and lunch menus.

She really shouldn't, but...

"Well, actually, I'd love a malt instead of coffee," she admitted.

Judging by the way she looked, Alec doubted that she indulged in too many of those. He nodded. "Sure, anything you want."

"And fries," Marissa added as Alec walked toward the counter.

He laughed. He'd pictured her as a health nut, dedicated to all things vegetable. It was nice to know he was wrong. Her tastes matched his own. "Healthy appetite."

She didn't know about healthy, but the appetite was certainly there. "I haven't had time to eat all day," she confessed. Ever so gently, she tucked the light blanket around her sleeping son, careful not to rouse him. "And while it might not be healthy, I've got to admit I do love junk food once in a while."

Well, at least she wasn't pretentious, but then, he'd already figured that out.

"Junk food it is." He glanced at the menu with its photos of popular combinations. "Do you want a burger with that?"

Yes, she did. But she didn't really want to eat alone. "Are you getting anything? Besides the coffee, I mean."

It had been a long time since he'd eaten in a place like this. The last time was probably while he was still in college. He'd shared a bag of fries with Christine. Memories of their days on campus came tiptoeing back to him. To his surprise, they didn't hurt quite so much as they once had.

"Sure," he said gamely. "Why not?"

The lanky youth behind the counter looked barely sixteen and was eager to please. The order was filled within less than three minutes. Alec smiled, remembering himself at that age. Had he really ever been that young? It almost didn't seem possible.

He ignored the change from his ten. "Keep it," he said, turning away from the counter.

Bewildered, the teenager stared at the money on the counter before he mumbled a thank-you and quickly shoved the change into his pocket.

Alec slid the tray onto the table in front of Marissa. Instinct had made him get an extra-large order of fries. He had a feeling that Marissa could more than do justice to it.

Sitting, he took his own drink and fries off the tray. He glanced at the two children.

"They're still asleep," he noted with relief. To him, it

was tantamount to a minor miracle. Andrea never fell asleep before nine.

Marissa stuck her straw into the hole she made in the plastic lid. Pink foam made an aborted attempt to escape. A little dribbled over onto the side. Marissa slid her finger along the container and licked it off. It tasted like heaven.

"The class tired them out." She took a sip and savored it. "That's the idea."

Damn stupid for a man to feel himself aroused because he watched a woman lick pink liquid off her finger. He wasn't accustomed to being stupid. Needing to look at something other than her eyes, Alec looked down at the printed message on the paper place mat. It gave details of Squirrely Joe's latest contest.

"And it's a great idea," he muttered, trying to get his mind on the conversation and not on the sensual curve of her mouth. "They look so peaceful like that."

He laughed to himself, remembering his mother's complaint when he had picked Andrea up this afternoon for class. Andrea had crawled over to Roberta's poodle and tried to take Robespierre's collar off to use as a teething ring.

"Hard to believe that they can cause so much damage when they're awake, when they look like that."

"It has to do with survival." She looked at Christopher as she unwrapped her hamburger. "God made them look so adorable so that we would forgive them for making us completely crazy."

Marissa took a bite and closed her eyes, savoring it. Lord, but it did feel good getting something into her stomach. It felt even better doing it sitting down. Lately, whenever she ate, it was either on the run or standing over the sink. A chair just didn't enter into the picture.

Alec couldn't take his eyes off her. To look at her face, you would have thought she was enjoying some painstakingly prepared gourmet meal instead of a plain hamburger that had been whipped up in minutes and took pennies to make.

After a beat, after that first initial hunger was appeased, Marissa could feel Alec's eyes on her, even though hers were still closed. She opened them, looking at him. Alec didn't look away. Instead he seemed rather amused. Marissa cocked her head, trying to guess what was on his mind.

"What?" She raised her napkin to her face. "Do I have catsup on my chin?"

He placed his hand over hers, lowering it. "No. I've just never seen anyone go into ecstasy over a hamburger before."

She laughed ruefully. "Sometimes I get so busy, I forget to eat. It's nice to be reminded." She allowed herself one more bite before she got down to business. Toying with a French fry, she raised her eyes to his. "So, what did you want to ask me about?"

He watched the fry disappear between her lips and had to rouse himself to recapture his train of thought.

"Monday, when I told you about my problem—finding a nanny," he added quickly when he realized that there was no reason in the world for her to remember their conversation. There were at least twenty-five other parents in the group.

"Yes?"

"You said something about letting me know if you ran across a suitable candidate. I'm still looking for someone to take care of Andrea while I'm at work and I'd much rather have a personal recommendation from you than study testimonials from strangers I don't know and will never meet." A disparaging smile hovered on his lips. "For all I know, the references could come from friends of the applicants."

"Sounds like you've been burned."

"Toasted to a crisp," he admitted. "I've had my share of bad nannies. And I only want the best for Andrea.

Marissa smiled at Andrea. With her light, wispy blond hair, she looked like daddy's little girl all the way. It was easy to see why he would dote on her. Marissa felt a pang she recognized as envy. It wasn't in the Sergeant's makeup to dote, or to do anything but criticize and register disapproval.

Raising her eyes to look at him, she asked, "Who watches her now, while you're at work?"

"Roberta."

He'd already indicated that he wasn't married. "Girlfriend?" she guessed. He probably favored someone tall and willowy. Blond, like his daughter and, probably, his wife.

Alec smiled to himself. Knowing Roberta, she probably would have liked to have heard that. He shook his head. "Mother."

She looked at him, stunned. "You call your mother Roberta?"

Taking another fry, he shrugged. "It's her name. And she insists on it. I haven't been allowed to call her anything else in years. She's not exactly the domestic type."

And he wasn't happy about that, Marissa thought, reading between the lines.

Alec twirled the straw between his thumb and forefinger, remembering the way Roberta had looked as he'd pulled out of the driveway this evening. She had given a performance worthy of Greta Garbo in *Camille* and twice as melodramatic. She couldn't take much more of this, she'd informed him. Andrea had almost given her and her beloved poodle a nervous breakdown.

"She gave me twenty-four hours to find a nanny." He lifted his eyes to hers. "So I was wondering if you knew of anyone at all who you might be able to recommend."

Marissa bit her lower lip, thinking. The classified section was once again sticking out of her purse, reminding her that she still hadn't had time to look through it. She had enough to deal with without trying to help Beckett with his problem, as well.

Unless...

Damn, how could she have been so thick? Being a nanny wasn't exactly what she was aspiring to, but it was a good deal more preferable than trying to share quarters with Jeremy, the man who couldn't take no for an answer, or hitting the bricks, looking for a place to stay and someone to share the rent with. Odds of finding a compatible roommate who didn't mind an overenergized eighteen-month-old getting into everything were rather slim to nonexistent.

If nothing else, it was worth a shot. She didn't have anything to lose. If things didn't work out, she would be no worse off than she was now. "You said the job was for a live-in?"

"That's what I'd prefer, but I'm flexible." Another word for desperate, he thought.

"Where would the nanny live, if she were to live in?" she pressed.

"I have a guest house. It's nothing big, but it would—"

He said something further, but Marissa had stopped listening.

A house. A guest house. That meant there had to be more than just one tiny bedroom. Christopher could have his own room rather than sleeping in what could have passed for a broom closet without the door. Hope burrowed into her breast and settled down for a long visit.

Marissa leaned forward. "Mr. Beckett, I think I might be able to solve your problem."

And mine.

Chapter Four

Things didn't just fall into place this well. Not for him. That would be too much to hope for. But what else could she mean?

"Are you telling me that you're going to take me up on my offer?"

Even as he said it, Alec could feel a sense of relief taking over. He wasn't going to have to sit through endless hours, trying to find the right person to look after his child after all. He would have kissed Marissa if he hadn't restrained himself at the last moment.

Funny how things never turned out quite the way you planned. She'd had the rest of the year all mapped out. And then a monkey wrench named Jeremy had fallen into the machinery. Still, things could be a lot worse. Beckett had walked into her life at just the right time.

She smiled at the incredulous expression on his face. He looked like a man who had just gotten all six numbers right on his lottery ticket and was afraid to look down at the stub again.

She put him out of his misery. "That's exactly what I'm telling you."

Thank God. Still, he was curious. "What made you change your mind?"

She shrugged, finishing off her malt. She pushed her straw through the hole and placed the empty container back on the tray.

She was stalling, he thought.

Marissa really didn't feel like getting into it. "Certain circumstances have changed since I last spoke to you."

She didn't strike him like the wavering type. He would have thought that once she made up her mind, she would stick by her decision. "What kind of circumstances?"

Friendly and outgoing, Marissa still didn't like to share pieces of herself with people. Private things were supposed to remain private. She supposed that was the Sergeant's training. The realization had her making an effort to ignore her natural tendencies. Besides, the man had a right to know a little background on the person he was entrusting his daughter to. She'd want to know things, if the tables were turned.

Marissa picked up the empty straw casing and began folding it back and forth like an accordion. She avoided his eyes. "I suddenly find myself without a place to live. Jeremy's coming home." The last was a throwaway line, said more to herself than to him.

"Jeremy?"

Was that her ex-husband? A lover? He hadn't thought of her as someone having a lover, only as this exuberant woman in bright-colored leggings. Of course, someone like her would have a lover. Women who looked like Marissa Rogers were at a premium, to be scooped up whenever they were unattached.

Marissa could tell by his tone that Beckett didn't understand. "It's not what you think. Jeremy is a friend of a friend who went to New York to work in an off-off-Broadway play.'' She repeated the term that Jeremy had bandied about cavalierly the night she moved in.

Alec found it amusing. "Off-off-Broadway?"

She nodded. "Off-off," she repeated. "Probably in Brooklyn. Anyway, he couldn't keep up payments on his apartment and rent one in New York, too, even if he was going to share the cost with roommates. So he sublet it to me. At the time he didn't expect to be back until the end of the year."

A rueful smile lifted the corners of her mouth, making her lips extremely appealing. He studied her as she spoke, not realizing that he was staring.

"I guess for him the year ended a little early." She blew out a breath. "The play closed yesterday. He has no other prospects, so he's coming home. He's supposed to get here by the end of the week. Which means I have to find a place to live by then."

She said it so lightly, he got the impression that it was actually no big deal. But it had to be if she was agreeing to become Andrea's nanny. Alec probed a little. By no means did he want to dissuade her. He just wanted to find out a little more about the situation. For Andrea's sake.

"You can't share expenses with him?"

She laughed. He didn't know Jeremy. "Expenses, yes, space, no." She remembered the last time she saw Jeremy—the only time they'd been alone. "Jeremy is a dancer and very agile."

He was lost. "What does that have to do with it?"

If he had been there, he would have understood. "Jeremy can seem as if he's in all places at the same time." Holding her hands up in front of her, she crossed and recrossed them, like an ancient magician weaving a spell. "Specifically, my place. My space. Believe me, if there was any way I could stay, I would. I hate giving up the apartment.''

"Nice area?" he guessed.

"Lovely area, but it's the convenience I'm thinking of. The apartment's near the college. I can almost tumble out the front door and get to class before the late bell rings." And some mornings, when things were particularly hectic, she really needed that proximity.

She didn't live far from him, Alec realized. It was a wonder their paths hadn't crossed until now. Bedford was a growing area, but it wasn't all that huge yet. They probably shopped at the same supermarket, he guessed. That practically made them neighbors.

"Well, I can't offer you that kind of convenience." He grinned, envisioning her rolling head over heels. It wasn't a stretch. He'd seen her tumbling on the trampoline with some of the older children. "Unless you don't mind tumbling for a while, but I am still pretty close to the college. I live in the Cedarwood development. My house overlooks the lake."

She'd driven through Cedarwood countless times to get to the bookstore. The local association made certain that the residents kept up their homes so they looked perpetually new. The result was a lovely community that was a pleasure on the eyes. It would be a great place for Christopher to live, she thought.

But something didn't sound quite right. "I don't remember those homes having guest houses."

"I had quarters added on over the garage and there's another room just behind it, connected by a stairway. The lot has an odd shape, so there was plenty of room for renovations." He planned to build a small playhouse in the backyard for Andrea in about a year or so, doing the work himself.

The houses in that area were all two stories. "Why would you have built extra quarters?"

Since they were finished eating, Alec rose and emptied

the tray in the receptacle behind them. "It was a studio once." He picked up the infant seat. Andrea stirred, pursing her lips as if she were sucking her bottle, but went on sleeping.

Slinging her purse over her shoulder, Marissa cradled Christopher in his seat and followed. "Oh? What kind of a studio?"

An image whispered across his mind. Christine at the easel, a smudge of paint on her hand. Blue. She'd referred to it by some artsy name when he pointed it out, but he didn't have a head for things like that. To him, blue was blue.

"Art studio. My wife painted." Alec pushed the door open with his back, then stood holding it until Marissa walked through.

She walked beside him to the car. "She doesn't paint anymore?" Stupid, Marissa chastised herself as soon as the question was out. Beckett was obviously talking about his ex-wife.

He looked down at Andrea as he tucked her seat into the rear of his car. "She doesn't do anything anymore."

There was no emotion in his voice. He might as well have been reciting lines out of a play he was reading. He didn't want to feel anything anymore. It was too exhausting.

Alec concentrated on strapping the seat in. "My wife died giving birth to Andrea. Complications. She started hemorrhaging and before they could stop it, she went into shock, and then cardiac arrest. They tell me that things like that are very rare." Finished, he straightened and looked directly into her eyes. His voice was hollow, divorced from the rest of him. The only indication that he felt anything at all was in his eyes. They were moist. "All it takes is once."

Oh, God, she had walked into that one with both feet. Marissa felt absolutely awful. Still holding Christopher and his seat against her, she touched Alec's arm in a mute gesture of comfort.

"Oh, Alec, I am so sorry. I didn't mean to pry." She bit her lip, wishing she could have bitten off her tongue. "I was just curious about the studio."

Her sympathy embarrassed him. He should have just passed off her question lightly, given her any answer, not played true confessions. But Alec hadn't known he was going to say what he had until the words were out. It wasn't her fault that her question had stirred up memories.

"That's all right, you didn't know." He helped her position Christopher's seat beside Andrea's. Alec had driven them to Squirrely Joe's. Marissa's car was still in the Y's parking lot. "Anyway, it was a lucky thing I had the studio added on. It's perfect for a live-in nanny. That way, we each have our privacy and yet you're right there when I need you."

He realized what that had to sound like as soon as he said it. Alec didn't want there to be any misunderstandings between them. "I mean, when Andrea needs you."

Alec held the passenger door open for her until she was seated. He seemed to be tripping over his own tongue a good deal tonight. But there was something about Marissa's sympathetic nature that drew the sentiments, more than the words, out of his mouth.

He was going to have to watch that.

Alec rounded the hood and got in behind the wheel. It had been a long time since he'd had anyone really listen to him. But then, he supposed it had been a long time since he'd attempted to share anything so personal. He firmly believed that some sentiments were best left on the shelf, under lock and key. It did no one any good to allow them into the light of day.

It wouldn't change anything.

She turned to look at him as he started the car. "Then you've raised Andrea all by yourself this past year?"

He hadn't meant to make it sound as if it had been a hardship. Andrea was the best part of his life. It was fatherhood that was still mystifying him. It probably always would.

"Not alone. Like I said, there've been nannies and I've persuaded Roberta to lend a hand on occasion." He smiled, thinking of his mother. "Although it's her housekeeper who does the actual changing and feeding. Roberta just chucks her under the chin and says a few baby talk syllables at her." His smile widened into a grin. "Andrea, not the housekeeper." He spared Marissa a glance as he eased into traffic. Dusk was settling in, bringing along a cool mist. He turned on the car's headlights and with them, the windshield wipers. They moved lazily across the glass, resting after every pass. "Don't misunderstand, my mother isn't a bad woman, she just has trouble giving of herself to anyone under the age of thirty."

He was probably close to that now himself, she guessed, although when he smiled, his face looked more boyish and rugged. "Then you're due soon?"

He laughed. She had a good eye. "In a few months."

How old was she? he wondered. "Is turnabout fair play?"

She arched a brow. "Excuse me?"

A trace of whimsy flittered through him. It passed so quickly that it didn't occur to Alec that it had been a year since he'd felt anything remotely similar. "Do I get to ask you your age?"

She lifted a shoulder indifferently. "No law against asking."

From her tone, he knew he could ask, but she wasn't going to answer. She'd said she was going for a masters, that had to put her at about—what?—twenty-five at the earliest. But she sounded a great deal more mature than that. He couldn't tell by looking at her. It aroused his curiosity. Most women didn't become secretive about their age until well into their thirties.

Alec stepped on the accelerator again. "I think I'll pass."

Marissa took pity on him. "I'm twenty-eight, but I would think it would be my experience rather than my age that would be more useful to you in ascertaining what sort of a woman you're hiring."

He switched the wipers on to a higher speed as a light sprinkling of rain was dotting the windshield. Twenty-eight. That would explain the maturity, though she didn't look her age. "I already know the kind of woman I'm hiring." He ticked off the attributes he'd observed and gleaned from their conversation. "A very energetic, capable one who evidently knows how to roll with the punches and has turned survival into an art form."

She laughed. "Wow, with a recommendation like that, I'd hire me, too." Turning in her seat, she leaned back to check on Andrea and Christopher. Both were still dozing. Luck was holding, but probably not for much longer. She raised her eyes to Alec's face. "Just how did you arrive at that glowing conclusion?"

He'd caught a whiff of something sweet and tangy when she inclined her head. It was vaguely familiar, but he couldn't place it. It took him a minute to focus on her question.

"Easy. You're good with kids, hence capable. You know how to roll with the punches because you're a single mother who's made a home for herself and her son, planning on a future rather than retreating into bitterness. And you're a survivor because here you are, taking advantage of an opportunity that you heretofore only thought was annoying."

Had she given him that impression? She hadn't meant to. "Not annoying, just not doable."

Alec looked at her. The light from the passing cars refracted through the wet windshield, dusting her skin with a sheen of diamonds. He found himself wondering about the man who left her. He must have been blind as well as insensitive.

"And now?" Alec pressed.

"Now I'm going to have to find a way to do it." She'd already begun to outline schedules in her head. "It's a matter of getting everything down on paper and seeing what can either be pushed aside, postponed or scaled down."

He was curious to hear just what she had decided to rearrange in her life. "Go on."

"All right. Priorities." She took a deep breath, visualizing a page in her mind. "In order to have a place to stay, I need to take care of your daughter. In order to continue receiving my scholarship money, I have to maintain twelve credits a quarter and a B average. Besides that, I do have a commitment to the Y to teach those Baby and Me classes. They already advanced me money against my wages so that I could buy a few things for Christopher." She saw the unspoken question in his eyes. "It was a rough winter."

"No child support?" He would have known he was stepping into territory that was best left unexplored had he thought about it. But it seemed a natural enough question when he asked.

"Some, but not much." She knew through mutual friends that Antonio was doing very well, but she refused to ask for more than they had originally agreed upon. It wasn't in her nature to beg. In that respect, at least, she was too much the Sergeant's daughter to sacrifice her pride. She'd just have to find a different way—and by accepting Beckett's offer, she had. "It never seems to be enough."

She glanced over her shoulder at her son. "Every time I turn around, Christopher's outgrowing something."

He was acquainted with that. But for him, it was never a hardship. He wondered how he would have managed if he'd not only needed a nanny, but the funds for one, as well.

"They do that," he agreed. Andrea had already grown so much in the last year that he couldn't think of her as a baby anymore. In a way, he rather missed that, the feel of something so tiny, so sweet curling up in the crook of his arm. He'd never thought of himself as a sentimental man until she had entered his life.

A thought occurred to Marissa. "Tell me something. Why haven't you thought of placing Andrea into a pre-school or a day-care center?" She knew that she would have been lost without the one that existed on campus. It allowed her to attend her Wednesday classes, which were only given in the daytime.

Was she changing her mind again? "I want someone who can give Andrea the attention she needs. I don't want her to be lost in a crowd, just one of the kids who's being cared for." His reasons were grounded in his own past and the myriad strangers who had taken care of him. "There'll be plenty of time for her to be melded into a crowd when she's older. Right now, I want someone who can focus on her, who's there for her when I can't be."

He paused at another traffic light. He seemed to be catching each one tonight, but for once he wasn't in a particular hurry. Talking to Marissa was pleasant, soothing. Alec placated his conscience, which directed his attention to all the office work he was leaving undone, by telling himself that he was actually conducting an interview. One interview instead of twenty.

"And you know, I can't think of anyone better than you." It was true. There was just something about her that told him she was the genuine article and that he was lucky that she had changed her mind. That Andrea was lucky, he amended silently.

Marissa wasn't accustomed to things being taken on faith. "Without checking out my references?"

He supposed it wouldn't hurt, but there would have to be something pretty damaging before he went against his instincts. "Do you have any?"

She flushed. The question had just come out. It had never occurred to her to garner any letters from the various places she had worked. "Just the school where I teach."

The answer was refreshingly honest. Other people might have tried to snow him, the way one applicant had. She'd had glowing letters to show him, none of which had checked out when he'd looked into them. It was obvious that the woman had thought he'd be so impressed with her references that he wouldn't think to question the people who supposedly wrote them.

"Then I guess I've checked out everything I need to." Andrea was beginning to make noises in her sleep. That meant she was going to be waking up soon. "Andrea likes you, and to me, that's the most important reference of all." He guided his car into the now-empty lot and parked next to hers. Pulling up the emergency brake, Alec turned to look at her. "So, do we have a deal?"

She'd learned to be cautious in her actions, no matter how blithely she appeared to be going through life. "Do I get to ask you any questions?"

Her response amused Alec. "You want to see my references?"

She'd seen and heard enough to form her own opinion about him. References were just nice pieces of paper that served as reinforcements of an opinion. If there was something damning about him, probably even his best friends wouldn't know.

"No, I just need to work out a few logistics with you and I thought we should do it up front. That means I need to know your schedule. I have evening classes on Monday, Tuesday and one on Thursday. On Wednesdays I have two during the day. Also, there are the classes I teach at the Y. You already know about the time. I can bring Andrea to those. You don't have to come along anymore if you don't want to. I'll keep an eye on her the way I do with Christopher."

He had no plans of dropping out. "Hey, I was just getting good at it." Or was there some sort of hidden message in her suggestion? He eyed her. "Wasn't I?"

She nodded. "You're one of the more attentive fathers. Actually," she admitted, "until I started teaching classes, I wasn't aware that fathers could be attentive."

Alec thought of his own father and drew the only logical conclusion he could. "Your father walk out when you were young?"

The assumption surprised her. Marissa shook her head. "A person doesn't have to leave not to be there," she said quietly. It was as much as she was willing to say on the subject. "So, what do you think? Can we work things out to our mutual satisfaction?"

There was no way he was going to let her out of it. Not when the alternative meant either going back to his mother or sifting through endless candidates who would probably leave him cold. Besides, she was going to be good for Andrea. He had a feeling.

"I'm home two days a week. One of those can be on Wednesdays. I can watch Christopher for you while you're attending class."

"You don't have to. There's a great day-care center on the campus." The center had its limits, one of which was that it closed at five. She bit her lip. "But the evenings—"

It took effort to draw his eyes away from her mouth. "All right, the evenings then."

"That would certainly make things easier," she admitted. Relying on Jane was an evening-to-evening thing. A few times Jane's mother had come to take her place because Jane had too much homework to watch Christopher. And there were times when she had to skip class because Jane and her mother were both unavailable and she couldn't find anyone to stay with Christopher. If she were living on Beckett's property, that problem would be solved. Provided Christopher didn't send the man running for the hills.

"So, we have a deal?" he prodded again, putting out his hand.

Marissa slipped hers into it. "We have a deal."

He felt relieved. He also felt something else, something nameless that was pushing its way forward, into the sun. Suddenly aware that he was holding her hand much too long, he released it. "How soon can you move in?"

She didn't even have to think. "As soon as I can get my things together. I don't have a class tonight, so I can pack and be over in the morning."

Now that the deal was sealed, he was anxious to remove any obstacles. He wouldn't feel secure until she was actually on the premises. "Why don't I come over and help you pack? Can you be over tonight?"

She looked uncertain. "Your car is too small. We'd have to make several trips."

"I have a van."

He certainly was determined, she thought, laughing. "Are you usually this pushy?"

"No, but I'm usually not this desperate, either," he confessed. "There's a meeting in the morning I have to attend and if I leave Andrea with Roberta for a third day in a row, she'll probably make me endure the death scene from *Hamlet* before letting me out the door."

He was exaggerating, but she found it rather cute. "Which one?"

Alec didn't have to think. He knew his mother. "All of them. She tends to be a little overly dramatic." He saw a skeptical look enter Marissa's eyes. "Roberta was in the theater when she was young. Younger," he amended, knowing that if his mother had heard him just then, there would have been hell to pay. "She claims it never leaves the blood."

His mother sounded eccentric. "You must have had an interesting childhood."

He lifted a shoulder. "That's one way to put it." But, if Marissa worked for him, she'd find out about Roberta soon enough. "It was unique. Roberta's family was, and is, well off. She is the family black sheep. But, since she was their only sheep, they doted on her and let her do whatever she wanted. Trouble was, she never quite knew what she wanted, other than to remain perpetually young." He recited the story from memory, having heard it from his grandmother a number of times. "She married my father against everyone's wishes, which was why I think she actually married him in the first place. As an act of rebellion, nothing more. By the time I was born, Roberta had declared herself out of love and had gone on to enroll in an 'acting school for talented beginners.' Her words, not mine. My father left. I was entrusted to a nanny while she went off to wow the world."

Marissa nodded, beginning to understand. "So, a tradition began."

He hadn't realized that was what it sounded like. "God, I hope not. I never want Andrea to feel the way I did."

She waited, but he wasn't going to tell her on his own. "How did you feel?"

"Like a pair of shoes someone wanted to keep polished in case they had to be brought out of the closet for some formal occasion but for the most part were kept pretty much out of sight.''

Her heart went out to the boy he had been. Feeling as if you didn't count was hell. ''Did you get along with your mother?''

Did he get along with her? Alec considered the question. He'd never had enough time alone with Roberta to really find out.

''I saw her infrequently. She was always going somewhere where she couldn't take me.'' After a while he'd stopped asking to be taken. ''And then she sent me off to boarding school so she wouldn't have to keep hiring nannies. They came and went with fair regularity.''

She could just see him, a lonely little boy, unloved, unnoticed. Invisible to the adults around him. In a way, they had a lot in common. ''That sounds absolutely terrible.''

He hadn't meant to bare this much of his past. There was absolutely no need for it. And yet a small part of him did feel better, sharing this. ''It sounds worse than it was. I managed to grow up and make something of myself and she likes to say she had a hand in it, when it suits her.''

And he lets her, even though he knows it isn't true, Marissa thought. That said a lot about him. ''But she won't let you call her mother.''

He shook his head. Roberta wouldn't answer if he did. ''Not since I became taller than she was. I was almost fifteen and home for Christmas when she told me she wanted me to start calling her Roberta.''

Merry Christmas. ''What about Andrea? Is she going to be able to call her Grandmother?''

Alec began to laugh, just picturing that. ''Not unless Andy wants that to be the last word she ever says. No, I expect Roberta will continue be 'Roberta' to all concerned.'' He'd said so much more than he had intended.

Alec looked at the woman beside him, bewildered. "How did we get started on this, anyway?"

She was the soul of innocence. "I asked you a question and it just came out."

He shrugged self-consciously. "I'm not accustomed to talking this much. It has to be something in the fries." He put the blame on the likeliest target. It was better than admitting that talking to her was a comfortable thing and words just seemed to slip out of their own accord.

Marissa nodded, her expression solemn. "I hear that the FBI has been known to use French fries when interrogating spies and trying to get international secrets out of them."

For a second he said nothing and she was afraid that she had gone too far and annoyed him. And then he laughed. "You have a smart mouth, you know that?"

She grinned. "Yes, I've been told that."

It was also a very tempting mouth, but he saw no reason to say that out loud. It was bad enough that he had thought it. It had absolutely no place in the relationship he saw for them.

"As long as you know. All right, here's the plan. You give me your address and I'll be back with the van within the hour." Within the half hour if everything went well, he added silently.

Marissa tore off a piece of the classified section and wrote her address in the margin. She wasn't going to be needing that paper anymore, she thought with satisfaction.

Chapter Five

Arms loaded down, Marissa moved aside a box that was in her way with the tip of her toe. With a heave, she dropped her belongings onto the king-size bed that dominated the small bedroom. Jeremy, she'd been told, spent a great deal of time in bed, entertaining. He didn't seem to mind the fact that there was hardly any space left over to maneuver within the room, but she did. It made packing a test of ingenuity.

Going into the closet again, she tried to decide what to take out next. The naked bulb that swayed slightly overhead each time she passed cast long, eerie shadows along the walls. That would have scared her out of her wits once, she thought. She'd spent a tortured childhood being afraid of the dark. The Sergeant had been totally unsympathetic, refusing to leave on a night-light for her.

"Damn waste of money. She's my daughter. She has no business being afraid of the dark and she isn't going to be. Not if I have anything to say about it." As if, she thought, shouting at her would make her brave.

Her mother had made a feeble attempt to talk the Sergeant into allowing her to leave on a light to chase away the shadows. It had fallen on deaf ears and she'd retreated, afraid to oppose her husband any further. Afraid not of physical reprisals, but verbal ones. The Sergeant's tongue was his sharpest weapon. So Marissa had spent many long nights lying awake, staring into the dark and waiting for the creatures to come out of hiding and get her.

They never did.

"Probably afraid to," she murmured. Her father cast a formidable shadow of his own. "You can have as many lights on to chase away the shadows as you want, Chris. I'll find a way to pay the electric bills." She smiled to herself. That was her main goal, to make Christopher's childhood one that he could look back on fondly. One that wasn't like hers.

Barren wire hangers dangled listlessly from the denuded rod. Marissa looked at the accumulated pile of clothing on the bed. There wasn't much there really, but then, she'd never paid that much attention to clothes, anyway. There were more important things in her life.

The most important of which was bouncing up and down within his playpen just outside the room. Marissa had dragged the playpen over so that Christopher could see her while she worked and, more importantly, so that she could see him. Lately, Christopher was turning into a budding escape artist. She was afraid that he'd find a way to climb out of the playpen and go scooting off. Thank God, he hadn't learned how to open doors yet.

Marissa pulled a large, flattened box from underneath the bed and opened it. She secured the sides with duct tape.

"I hope I'm not doing anything we're both going to regret," she said as she started piling her books into the box. "But he does seem very nice and we do need a place to stay. Besides—" she couldn't resist running her hand over Christopher's head "—I think Andrea has a crush on you. You be nice to her, you hear? Don't break her heart too soon." She smiled at her son, at his perfect little features. Did all mothers think their sons were so handsome? "You are going to be a heartbreaker, you know. Girls are going to be beating down the door to get at you. We're going to have to work on a disguise to hide you from them."

"Hi-hi!" Christopher cried, bouncing.

"That's right, hide." He was learning how to communicate fast.

Fast. She sighed, gathering another armload of books. Beckett moved fast, she thought. She usually did, too. But maybe this time, it was a mistake. Maybe she should have stopped long enough to really think it over.

But then, she mused, reaching up to the top shelf, what she'd said to Christopher was true. She really didn't have much choice.

"I suppose I could always drop out and get a full-time job." It was a definite possibility, but one that was crushing to even mention. "But then I couldn't be around you that much. And we're so close to our goal, Christopher. Just two more months and Mommy's got her degree." Dropping five more books into the box, she glanced over her shoulder. Christopher wasn't even looking in her direction. "Not very impressed, are you?"

Christopher was too busy trying to chew off the strap that held up his rompers. There were drool marks all down the bibbed front. Five minutes into clean clothes and he looked a mess. Her own little dirt magnet, she thought fondly.

"You can't be hungry, I just fed you." She stopped packing her books and came over to the playpen. Marissa crouched to look at him more closely. "Are you teething again?"

Her hand under his chin, she tried angling his head, urging his lips apart with the tip of her finger pressed at the corner of his mouth. Gleefully, Christopher clamped his lips together even tighter.

"Come on, open up for Mommy, honey," she coaxed. Nothing. "You open up for every dust bunny and dirty thing you find on the floor, open up for me."

As if he understood every word she was saying and chose to ignore them, Christopher kept his mouth firmly shut.

"So, you're a little rebel already, huh?" She let go of his chin. God, but she loved this little human being who had been dropped into her life. "All right, be that way. You're probably not teething, anyway. You're not nearly vocal enough."

Each tooth that had appeared in his head had been heralded in with screams, endless crying and a convoy of sleepless nights.

Marissa looked up sharply at the sound of the doorbell. She rose, dusting off her knees. "Is he here already?" Suddenly edgy, she wiped her hands on the back pockets of her jeans. "He really must live close by."

Christopher had no opinion on the matter. He was back to testing the integrity of the netting on his playpen.

Crossing to the door, she took a deep breath and then threw it open. Alec was standing on the threshold, looking only slightly more casual than he had in class. Obviously he thought there was a dress code for helping someone move.

She grinned, wondering if the man ever got messy. She was sure Christopher could give him pointers in that.

"Hi."

She had a smudge on the tip of her nose. Alec squelched the unexpected, intense urge to brush it off for her with his thumb. That seemed much too personal.

"You should always look through the peephole before opening the door." If his tone was a tad gruff, it was himself he was annoyed with, not her.

"That would be difficult—" Marissa closed the door as he walked in "—without a peephole."

A woman who lived alone should have enough sense to be more cautious. "If you don't have a peephole, how do you know who's knocking?"

"Simple. I open the door."

He shoved his hands into his back pockets. She and her son were becoming part of his life, at least peripherally, and that made this his business, he rationalized.

"To anyone?"

She didn't have to think about her answer. "Pretty much. Bedford's a nice little town." That was why she'd come back here after her divorce. Because she'd liked it here so much, felt safe here.

Was she as innocent as she sounded? Alec wondered. She was an army brat and they were supposed to grow up faster than most. More savvy of the darker side of life. Obviously she was the exception. "Even nice little towns have their weirdos."

She knew what was bothering him. He was afraid that she would be cavalier about his daughter's safety. Marissa stopped him before he got any further. "You have a peephole?"

He didn't see what that had to do with anything. "Yes."

She inclined her head. "Then we don't have a problem. I'll use it." Case closed. Marissa looked around, suddenly realizing that Alec had returned alone. "Where's Andrea? You didn't leave her in the van, did you?"

"No, I left her with Roberta." Having Andrea along would have made helping Marissa move almost impossible.

She didn't understand. Beckett had specifically said that his mother had given him an ultimatum. "I thought—"

Alec knew what she was going to say. Roberta had looked stunned at his reappearance tonight. He'd quickly dissolved any protests by telling her about Marissa.

"I told her I'd hired a nanny for Andrea and that I had to help her move in. Roberta was so glad I'd found someone, she didn't realize that I was leaving Andrea with her for a couple of hours until I was at the door." He hadn't tried to put anything over on his mother. He valued his daughter's well-being far too much to just dump Andrea and run. "Besides, Dorothy's there."

"Dorothy?" Was that another relative?

He squatted beside the playpen. With his hands wrapped around the edge as he bounced, Christopher looked more than capable of bringing the whole thing down.

"Hi, big guy." He glanced at Marissa, answering her question. "Roberta's housekeeper. Dorothy loves kids. In small doses."

He rose, ruffling the boy's dark hair. It felt silky. Absently he wondered if Christopher got that from his mother. Did hers feel as silky?

And what the hell did that have to do with anything?

Marissa nodded. "That's usually true of most people."

He looked at her, remembering the genuine joy in her eyes when she worked with the toddlers in class. "But not you."

"No, not me." Her mouth curved. "I was the oldest in my family. Five brothers and sisters, all born yelling."

"I would have thought having to take care of them would have made you sick of kids."

Marissa grinned. "You would, wouldn't you?" It had had just the opposite effect. She loved children, all children. If raising Willie, her youngest brother and Christopher's prototype, hadn't turned her off on the whole breed, nothing ever would. "But being responsible for them gave me a feeling of stability, a sense of home, even on the road. You don't get that very much when you're an army brat.''

She was digressing, she thought. And telling him too much. Hooking her thumbs in the loops of her jeans, she rocked on the balls of her feet as she looked up at Alec. "So, have you brought your muscles?''

She had an unsettling way of jumping from one thing to another. He wondered if a short attention span was catching. His own mind kept hopping around whenever he was around her. Some of the hops were beginning to bother him. "Excuse me?''

Marissa indicated the two large cartons she had just filled. "Some of these boxes of books are pretty heavy. And, as you might have noticed, I'm on the second floor.''

"Yes, I did notice that.'' Walking up the stairs, he'd begun to have second thoughts about volunteering so quickly.

Putting a little space between them, Alec looked around the apartment. There wasn't much in the way of furniture, but the room wasn't empty by any means. There were knickknacks, mementos probably, scattered about, giving the room a warm touch. Mostly, though, it was crammed with toys. Toys, a playpen, a wind-up swing and several other things whose sole function was to make Christopher's life more pleasant.

Alec eyed the sofa. A neutral beige that was amazingly clean given Christopher's penchant for wiping his hands on any surface, the sofa was long and chunky. It was going to be a bear to get down the stairs, even with help.

He could feel his back aching already. Maybe he would just hire a moving company for her. "How much of this is yours?''

"Only the Lilliputian stuff.'' She gestured toward the wind-up swing in the corner. "All the furniture belongs to Jeremy.''

Never mind the movers. This was going to be a piece of cake. "You travel light."

She shrugged. That had been from necessity. Necessity and a lack of funds. "You pick up a few things as an army brat." Taking the duct tape, she swiftly taped shut all four drawers of Christopher's bureau. "Never get attached to anything more than you can carry away with you."

That sounded like a Spartan philosophy. He wondered how much of it was her and how much had been her father's doing. "What about Christopher's things?"

He'd caught on to her one weakness. "There are exceptions."

Alec found himself being amused. And charmed. There was a danger in that, but he felt he was in control of the situation. "Got an answer for everything?"

"Pretty much." Her eyes danced as she said it.

"Well, let's get to it." He looked around. "What do you want to move first?"

"Doesn't matter. How about the books?" She led the way into the bedroom. Ordinarily, she hated moving. It dredged up too many painful memories. This time, though, the memories were muted, fading into the background in the face of new possibilities.

It was going to be all right, she thought. She hadn't been sure until just now, when he'd stopped to ruffle Christopher's hair. Watching had given her a warm, secure feeling. It was a sign.

Marissa indicated the boxes. "Lucky thing I never threw out the cartons."

Squatting, Alec slid his hands around the base of the carton. "Lucky," he grunted, struggling to his feet.

She felt guilty. "Do you want any help with that? I'm stronger than I look."

He'd watched her in class. If strength had anything to

do with stamina, she'd convinced him. But there was such a thing as too many hands in a project.

Alec shook his head. "If you try to help, we're both liable to fall down the stairs."

She raised her hands in the air. "I never said a word. Just be careful, okay?" The last thing she wanted was for him to get hurt because he was helping her move.

Marissa hurried over to the door and held it open for him. Alec shifted the carton, using his hip for leverage. He looked in. All the spines were neatly turned in one direction. Textbooks, every one of them. And all secondhand, judging from their condition.

"Have you read all of these?"

"Every last one of them."

There was no missing the pride in her voice. "Pretty dry reading."

Standing beside him, she rose on her toes and peered down on them. She couldn't resist running her hand along the books. "Not really. Actually, most of them are rather fascinating. A few, of course, I plan to use as doorstops. But they're all required reading." She closed the lid, patting it into place. "I don't like to throw out books." She looked up at him. "Seems wasteful."

Her cologne was beginning to infiltrate his system. It hadn't seemed nearly so potent before.

He forced his mind back on the topic. From what he could see, all her books dealt with psychology. "Do you ever read anything else?"

Reading was her passion, right after Christopher and kids in general. "Anything I can get my hands on. I just can't afford to buy them, that's all. It's the public library for me. They usually like their books back."

The sound of rain hitting the tile roof registered. She looked outside and saw that the light drizzle had transformed into a full-fledged storm.

Alec began to walk past her. She caught his arm. "Wait," she cried.

Did she want to pile something else on top? "I can't carry any more at one time."

But she had already darted inside. The next moment she reappeared with an umbrella. Marissa pressed a button at the base and it bloomed above their heads like a navy blue sunflower.

"The least I can do is try to keep you dry," she explained.

Having her hover over him was only going to slow him down. "A little rain never hurt anyone."

She was adamant. When he started for the stairs, she was right there with him. "That's what Noah's father-in-law said just before the deluge hit."

"Noah's father-in-law?" Alec didn't know whether to be amused by this elfin woman who was jockeying for position beside him or a little leery of her. "I never knew Noah had a father-in-law."

"Not after the rains hit. That's my point." She grew serious. "This is perfect weather to get sick in." Marissa held the umbrella high, attempting to protect as much of Beckett as she could.

The stairway was just wide enough to accommodate them. With the carton of books added in, the passage was tight. He could feel her body lightly brushing against his as they made their way down to ground level. She seemed oblivious to the fact that she was rubbing against him every step of the way.

But he wasn't oblivious, and that, he knew, wasn't a good thing. It had been a long time since he'd been aware of a woman as a woman. He didn't particularly want to be made aware of that anytime soon.

Still keeping the umbrella raised, Marissa looked around. "Is that your van?" There was a large, dark green vehicle parked against the curb, its rear facing the cluster of apartments.

He'd left it as close to her apartment as possible. "That's it."

His fingers were beginning to slip. Alec fervently hoped he could make it to the van without dropping the box. Puddles were beginning to form on the asphalt, capturing the glow of the street lamps in its dark pools. He didn't want the carton landing in one of them.

Moving ahead of him quickly, Marissa tried the van doors. They were unlocked. She opened one just in time for Alec to slide the carton in along the floor. Pushing it in farther, he closed the door and turned toward her. She was still holding the umbrella over him. "How many more of those?"

She grinned. "Cartons with books? Just one more. I've got to pack up my clothes, but we've still got to move Christopher's bureau, his crib, his high chair, toys, clothes..."

He held up his hand, stopping her. "I get the picture." She'd only mentioned the baby's things. "No TV set? No stereo?"

"No money," she countered.

It didn't seem to bother her, he thought, not having any possessions. Though she spoke lovingly of stability, Marissa reminded him of a free spirit, unencumbered by things. He found that rather appealing. Probably because it meant he didn't have that much to move, he rationalized.

Marissa surprised him by hooking her arm through his. When he looked at her quizzically, she urged him back to the apartment. "I don't want to leave Christopher alone for more than a few minutes."

It had only been less than three and he was in his playpen, but she didn't believe in taking foolish chances if she could help it. Not when it came to her son.

Alec let her lead the way, thinking it safer to remain in the rear rather than to make the trip up side-by-side again.

He thought wrong.

A rear view was just as unsettling in its own way as having her body move innocently along his had been. There was no doubt about it, the lady was in great shape. It would make keeping up with Andrea easier.

Although, Alec was beginning to get the feeling, that was probably the only thing that was going to get easier for him.

Just as she opened the door, Marissa heard a thud and then a laugh of glee from within. She hurried into the room just in time to scoop Christopher up. He was on the other side of the playpen and, from his expression, hell-bent for mayhem.

Alec stared at the empty playpen. "Wasn't he just in there?"

Marissa laughed, relieved that she had got here in time. She kissed Christopher's soft little cheek. It was sticky. Now what had he found to get into?

"Yes, he was. We're just going to have to call you Houdini from now on, Chris." She turned to look at Alec. "Last night I woke up to find that he had managed to get out of his crib." Thank God she was a light sleeper. "And he was so proud of himself." She nuzzled the boy in her arms. "Weren't you?" He giggled and she nuzzled his neck harder, eliciting an entire peal of squeals. "Weren't you?"

Alec looked on, thinking how nice it had to be, to feel that sort of love surrounding you. Christopher was one lucky kid. Alec would have gladly given his soul if his own mother had been only a tenth as attentive as Marissa when he was growing up.

"Why don't you hang on to David Copperfield there and

I'll take the last box down?'' He passed her, walking into the bedroom.

Marissa looked after him. "But it's still raining," she protested.

Hefting the carton, Alec came out of the bedroom. This one felt even heavier than the first had. It took effort not to grimace.

"I promise not to drown until I get your books into the van."

She placed Christopher back in the playpen. "I wasn't worried about the books."

He paused, leaning the carton against the wall and using it as a buffer. "You don't have to worry about me, either."

Cheerfully, she dismissed his words. "Sorry, it's not something I can turn on and off. I worry about people."

He knew he shouldn't go any further with this, but he did. "In general?"

"Yes."

Her answer surprised him. It should have made him feel better. He wasn't exactly sure why it didn't. "Then, I suppose it's all right. As long as it's nothing personal."

Marissa cocked her head, intrigued. "And if it were?"

His eyes were solemn. "That wouldn't be a good thing."

He was putting her on notice, she thought. "Duly noted." Out of the corner of her eye, Marissa saw Christopher begin a second attempt to escape his prison by using blocks for stepping stones. She removed them. "Stay put," she warned her son.

Alec shook his head. "And if I said the same thing to you?"

Marissa ignored him as she crossed to the door, umbrella in hand. "You're not paying me yet, so I don't have to listen." One hand on the umbrella, she gestured for Alec to walk out first.

Something told him that whether or not he paid her had

nothing to do with it. Marissa Rogers did what she wanted when she wanted. He wondered if hiring her and bringing her into his life was such a good idea after all.

But he had made a commitment and right now he had no other recourse. He only hoped, as he caught another whiff of her fragrance, that he wouldn't wind up regretting this somewhere down the road.

Chapter Six

The scent roused him, creeping into his dreams like a thief and stealing sleep away, bringing his body to attention before his mind was ever engaged.

At first it was her scent. Marissa's. The one he'd just barely detected last night in the car. Sweet, tangy, arousing. A scent to make a man dream of lying in a lush green meadow and of a woman to lay beside him.

Gradually, the scent faded, to be replaced by another stronger one that called to him almost as urgently, addressing other parts, other hungers.

Coffee.

He had to be hallucinating.

There was no other word for it. Why else would he be smelling the rich, wonderful aroma of coffee? He had to be hallucinating. Either that, or his dreams had suddenly taken on the parameters of virtual reality.

In either case, he was awake now. Wide awake. Alec glanced at the clock. Awake a full twenty minutes before the alarm was scheduled to go off. Well, schedule or not, he might as well get up.

Scrubbing his hands over his face slowly, Alec reluctantly surrendered the last dregs of sleep and sat up. As he did, he felt a sharp twinge in his back. Served him right for trying to do too much last night. He should have waited, maybe called Steve or Nat to come help him with the heavier pieces. An unexpected streak of machismo had urged him to do it himself, despite common sense and the rain.

Maybe he'd just been showing off, he mused. Behaving like a teenager again instead of a responsible man on the inside track of thirty.

In any event he'd done it, he'd gotten all of her things out of the apartment. He'd even managed to get Christopher's chest of drawers down the stairs and, with Marissa's help, into the van, before the rains suddenly turned torrential. The chest of drawers was the last, and heaviest, piece. They'd packed up the crib first, but it was a collapsible one and much easier to carry in comparison.

Because the rain refused to let up through the remainder of the evening, moving her things out of the van and into the guest quarters was temporarily postponed. Marissa had taken out only what she needed for the night. Since the quarters were furnished, she and Christopher had spent the night on the bed. She'd assured Alec that there was no need to bring up the crib until after the monsoon was over.

He'd been greatly relieved to hear that. Leaving Marissa to get acquainted with her new surroundings, Alec had gone to Roberta's to pick up his daughter. With his last shred of energy, he'd put Andrea to bed.

Placing one exhausted foot in front of the other, he'd fallen into bed himself, asleep before he hit the pillow. His last thought had been about Marissa, wondering how she liked her new home.

He'd only been vaguely aware that he had substituted the word home for quarters.

Miraculously, Andrea had let him sleep through the night

by doing the same. She'd seemed so full of energy when he'd picked her up at Roberta's, he'd been afraid she'd be up all night. But as if sensing that he wasn't up to dealing with any prolonged problems, Andrea had settled in and fallen asleep almost as quickly as he had.

It had been a night for miracles, he thought, getting out of bed.

He could swear that the scent of coffee was following him like a haunting refrain, but that was probably just brought about by wishful thinking. He would have killed for a good cup right now.

He also wished that he could rid himself of the lingering effect of his dream, but it slipped around him like an invisible, slick coating, refusing to disappear completely.

He'd dreamed of a woman, a woman whose face he couldn't make out. A woman whose laughter seemed to seep into his soul, unsettling him. Warming him. At first he thought he was dreaming of Christine again. He'd dreamed of her almost every night when she had first died. But that had slowly abated until, eventually, the dreams had stopped altogether.

This one wasn't about Christine. It was about someone else.

Someone, he told himself, he'd probably seen in a movie or a TV commercial. There was no use dwelling on it. It would go away on its own. Even now, the effects seemed to be fading a bit.

Alec showered and shaved in less than fifteen minutes. Getting dressed only took another five. Throughout it all he was amazed that there was still no sound from Andrea's room.

Maybe she was sick. He frowned, taking his jacket with him as he left his bedroom. Great way to break in the new nanny, leaving her with a sick baby.

Maybe he'd cancel his meeting today and stay home with

her. If Andy was sick, she'd need him. He tucked his tie under his collar, smoothing it down.

Damn, he couldn't cancel. There were buyers flying in from all over the country, not to mention an important backer, and he was one of the principle presenters. Murphy's law. He was on the cusp of a marathon week and a half with a sick baby on his hands. Thank God, he'd found Marissa in time.

Knotting his tie, he walked into Andrea's room. Maybe he was just overreacting. He supposed it was to be expected. Some of Roberta's blood did run in his veins. Maybe Andy had suddenly begun to sleep late.

"Up and at 'em, Andy. Time to get up."

Alec stopped abruptly. Andrea's crib was empty.

Instantly he thought the worst. Life had done that to him. He remembered reading about a man breaking into a home while a family was at dinner and trying to abduct one of the children right in front of everyone. What if someone had snuck in during the night and taken Andrea while he was sleeping in the next room?

Hurrying down the stairs, Alec was almost at the front door, on his way to get Marissa, when the smell of food finally registered.

Bacon. Fresh coffee. Someone was cooking. He sincerely doubted that the kidnapper had stopped to fix himself something to eat.

Relief warred with disbelief as Alec retraced his steps and turned toward the kitchen. He found Marissa there, with three frying pans on the stove, all going at the same time. Both children were up, dressed and seated in high chairs that were strategically separated just far enough so that neither could reach the other.

For a moment all Alec could do was stand there, looking. Being grateful and feeling just a little bit foolish. It had to be the stress of the past few months catching up to him and throwing his imagination into overtime.

This was one story he wasn't about to share with anyone in the office.

Frying pan in hand, poised over a plate, Marissa looked up to see Alec standing in the doorway, watching her. How long had he been there? She quickly transferred food from all three pans onto two plates and deposited the pans into the sink.

She smiled at him brightly. "Good morning."

Her greeting was cheerful and sweet enough to be poured over pancakes. Alec walked in, feeling as if he had just entered someone else's dream.

"Good morning," he echoed. He eyed the pans. "What are you doing?"

She took out two sets of knives and forks. The children had already been fed and were now playing with their empty dishes, finger-painting with what was left on their trays.

"My job. Did you forget? You hired me last night." She set a glass of orange juice in front of him.

She was making herself at home almost too easily, moving around his kitchen as if she'd always been here. None of the other women he'd hired before Marissa had fit in nearly half so well. He wasn't entirely certain if he could adjust to that.

"Yes. To watch Andrea," he reminded her. Not to double as a cook.

"Well, there she is." Marissa gestured grandly toward the little girl, an amused smile playing on her lips. "I'm watching her."

That wasn't all she was doing. Stimulated by the aroma, his mouth was beginning to water. "What's that wonderful smell?"

She smiled. There was nothing like being busy in the

kitchen first thing in the morning. It gave her a sense of being in control and calmed her. "Breakfast."

Yes, it certainly was, he thought, looking down at the plate she placed in front of him on the table. He'd come to regard one slice of toast, usually burnt, as breakfast. This was close to a feast as far as he was concerned.

"That wasn't part of your job," he stated.

She couldn't tell if he was pleased or annoyed. Well, at least he wasn't demanding, she thought.

"No, but I was sort of hoping that eating was." Marissa put out a second plate for herself. "You were asleep and I didn't want to bother you with every little detail. So I just got Andrea dressed, then brought her down for breakfast with Christopher."

He looked at the empty plates. Christopher was about to wear his. Marissa pried the food out of his fingers and gave him a piece of her French toast. Christopher began squeezing it.

Alec raised his eyes to hers. "They've already eaten?"

"Most of it. They insisted on wearing what didn't make its way into their mouths." A towel was carelessly slung over one of her shoulders. The edge had several stains derived from cleaning up Andrea's and Christopher's breakfasts. "I decided to have breakfast myself. I made you some while I was at it."

Alec appreciated it, but he didn't want her to think he expected her to do this all the time. "You didn't have to."

"No extra trouble. It is your refrigerator." She moved the plate of French toast, eggs and bacon a little closer to him. "You do like to eat in the morning, don't you?"

Alec sat down as if his knees had suddenly lost the ability to lock. The aromatic fragrance had completely undone him. Or was that the scent she was wearing? It mingled with something that was already growing murky and distant in his mind.

"I do, but I'd given it up. I never seemed to be able to cook and get Andy ready at the same time."

She wondered if he took catsup with his eggs. She hoped not. It would spoil the subtle flavoring she'd added. "Well, now you won't have to. I love to cook and you have a wonderful kitchen. It's so roomy."

As if to demonstrate, Marissa turned completely around, her arms outstretched. He thought he was watching Julie Andrews in the opening credits of *The Sound of Music.* Any second, he expected her to burst into song. But all she did was pour him a cup of coffee.

There was no "all" about it. The coffee, black as the darkest shade of velvet, tasted just as smooth as he sampled it. He could feel the caffeine kicking in instantly.

He almost drained his cup. It was heavenly. Setting it down, he looked at her, astonished. "Where did you learn how to make coffee like this?"

Her eyes shone. "The day I was born, one of the three fairies standing over my bassinet said a spell over me. She promised I would always be able to make wonderful coffee and bring strong men to their knees with it."

"Let me guess. *Sleeping Beauty.*" He finished the cup. "I can believe it. This is probably the best coffee I've ever had."

"Well, then, have some more." Marissa refilled his cup, then poured some for herself. "Actually, I picked up a little secret to making it, in Turkey."

He couldn't place what gave it that extra rich flavor. "What is it?"

She smiled mischievously. "If I told you, it wouldn't be a secret now, would it?"

"Turkey," he repeated. "Really?"

She nodded. Andrea dropped her spoon. It bounced on the floor and went under the table. Marissa bent to pick it up. "Part of my father's travels around the world."

Maybe that was why she could adapt to her surroundings so well. It was ingrained. Alec wondered if she'd liked all that uprooting and traveling. It would have been hell for him.

"Must have been hard on you, moving from place to place."

"It was." She wiped off Andrea's spoon with her napkin and gave it back to the girl. "But I got used to it. It was either that, or shrivel up." She shrugged good-naturedly. "I had brothers and sisters to take care of, so there was no time to think about how lonely I was. Besides, with them around, I wasn't all that lonely." They'd all taken their cue from her, so she'd had to maintain a cheerful facade. She'd done it so well, she wound up fooling herself in the bargain. Marissa's smile faded a little as she remembered. "It was harder on my mother."

"Didn't she have those same brothers and sisters to take care of? And you?"

It was too long a story to get into, even if she wanted to share it. But she was protective of those she loved, even if they were blemished.

"She had a lot in common with your mother. I don't think she was meant to be one. It was just something that happened." Her tone was matter-of-fact. Most of the scars had long since healed. She saw things differently now. "Actually, I happened." She avoided his eyes, although she felt them on her. "My father did the 'honorable' thing at the time and married her. I don't think either one of them ever forgave the other, or me, for that."

Alec started to say something, but she didn't want him to. She shouldn't have said anything. "So, how is it?" She nodded at his plate.

Above everything else, he could respect privacy. The meal was a nice, neutral topic. "Excellent. It's all excellent." He finished off the French toast. "If I hadn't hired you as a nanny, I would have begged you to become my cook.''

"Do you have one?" He hadn't mentioned any other people living here or coming in during the day, but then, maybe that was something he didn't think he had to tell her about.

"No," he laughed. He was only speaking figuratively. He was a fair enough cook to take care of his own needs, and Andrea's. With her it was still mostly a matter of heating up jars of baby food.

Because he didn't ask, she volunteered. She liked having a choice. "You do now. For the duration of our working relationship," she added in case he thought she was moving a little too quickly. He had looked uneasy, finding her here.

Alec sat back to look at her. She was rather an amazing woman. "You intend to be a nanny, teach classes, take classes, be a mother *and* cook?"

He did make it sound a little overwhelming, but then, the impossible always had an appeal for her. "Yes, and in the afternoon, I'll bend steel in my bare hands and juggle apples with my feet."

Alec laughed and some of the tension left his body. "I'd like to see that."

"I'll let you know when the next show is." Finished, she picked up her plate and put it in the sink. "By the way, I've worked up a schedule for us. It's posted on the refrigerator." Busy washing off the plate, she nodded toward the appliance.

Us.

Why did that have such a comfortable sound to it? It shouldn't. They were practically strangers, and besides, he knew better than anyone that you couldn't get comfortable about things. When you did, your guard was down and that was when life came and hit you between the eyes with a two-by-four.

The way it had when Christine died.

He'd learned the hardest way a man could that it was best never to allow yourself to get comfortable.

Alec crossed to the refrigerator and perused the list. It encompassed all of her hours and different activities, working Andrea's needs into it. She'd been thorough. "You did all this this morning?"

"Last night," Marissa corrected, wiping her hands on the towel. "I couldn't sleep, so I figured I should do something useful while I was up."

"I see." She was obviously what someone had been thinking of when they'd coined the word workaholic. "Well, you could have started making me a car."

She never missed a beat. "Sports car or sedan?"

He went back for a third cup of coffee, knowing he could have easily finished off the pot. "Don't you ever kick back, just sit still?"

That was for idlers, for people without a plan. Her father's daughter had to have a plan. He'd drummed that into her head early.

"What for? Life is to be used. And there's always so much to do. Somehow, it would seem wasteful to just sit and vegetate."

"I believe the word is rest."

It wasn't in her nature to be idle. "You rest, I'll do. That's what you're paying me for." She grinned, looking at him. She had to admit that he had made resting look rather appealing.

There was a strange glint in her eyes he couldn't read. "What?"

Marissa shook her head, but the smile remained. "Nothing." They were both better off if he didn't know that she had looked in on him when he was sleeping.

Alec studied her expression. She had *something* on her

mind. He could tell by her smile. "If you're working for me, you have to know that I appreciate complete honesty."

He wasn't going to like this. "All right, you asked for it. You look cute 'resting.' Sleeping, actually," she amended.

A brow rose in surprise. "When did you—"

She was quick to explain before he could jump to a conclusion. "I got the rooms confused. I thought yours was Andrea's and I walked in before I realized my mistake. I walked right out again," she added hastily. But not before the sight had managed to tug at her heart.

Then it hadn't been a dream. There had been a woman in his room. Now that he thought about it, the woman he'd thought he dreamed about had looked a great deal like Marissa. There'd been a reason for that. It *had* been Marissa.

He'd felt guilty having a sensual dream about a woman other than his wife. Now he knew he wasn't to blame. She'd been there and her cologne had done the rest. He was innocent.

Or as innocent as a man could be with someone like Marissa around. She had a way of awakening so many dormant feelings. Feelings he wanted to remain dormant, he reminded himself.

She bit her lower lip, waiting to see if he was annoyed about the unintended intrusion. He certainly looked as if something was on his mind. "I guess I should say I'm sorry I walked in like that. I didn't mean to."

"Then why are you grinning like that?"

"It's because, seeing you like that, you reminded me so much of Willie."

"Willie?" The name meant nothing to him.

"My youngest brother," she explained. "His hair always fell into his eyes just like yours did, like a sheepdog's, when he slept." It had been all she could do to not gently push his hair back from his face, the way she'd always done with Willie.

She missed Willie, missed the lot of them, she thought. Her brothers and sisters were scattered throughout the country now, each having staked out a different state. They'd slipped away from the family, one by one, like tears in the wind. Letters just weren't the same.

Rousing herself, Marissa looked Alec up and down. "I have to admit, you look a great deal more formidable dressed."

A tad self-conscious, he straightened his tie. "I hope so. I have to address several dozen people today. I wouldn't want any of them to think of me as a 'cute sheepdog.'"

Her eyes danced as she smiled. "Not to worry." She picked up his plate and deposited it into the sink. Christopher was beginning to make a fuss, beating his spoon against the high chair's tray. She coaxed it out of his greasy little fingers and then began to wipe them. "What is it you do, anyway?"

There were a lot of different facets to his job, but he summarized it for her, giving her the condensed version. "I develop software. Half the time I market it, as well." No one knew the product he created as well as he did. It was only logical from Rex's standpoint, that he be the one to make presentations to the various buyers.

She would have thought that either one would have been enough to keep him busy. "Aren't they both full-time jobs?" Marissa caught Andrea's bowl before it hit the floor.

"Nice save." He considered her question. Talk about the pot calling the kettle black. "At times. I guess that gives us something in common."

She smiled at him, feeling something warm and rosy growing within her. "I guess it does."

Alec looked at his watch. "Well, I'd better get on the road. Traffic is liable to be a bear." He had a short distance to travel, but he was taking no chances. There was a lot riding on this meeting.

She needed a phone number before he left. "Where can I reach you? If I need to call, I mean."

Alec took a business card from his wallet and gave it to her. "That's the number at work, but I'm going to be in a meeting all day, so you probably won't be able to get me." He flicked a finger down Andrea's nose and laughed as she wrinkled it and giggled. "If it's an emergency, have them page me."

Marissa tucked the card into her back pocket. "Will do." He began to leave. She surprised Alec by following him to the door. "Knock 'em dead."

Alec stopped and looked at her before picking up his briefcase. It had been a long time since he'd left the house with a woman's well-wishes ringing in his ears. It stirred a longing within him for things that no longer were.

"I'll do my best," he told her quietly.

She'd touched a sensitive spot, Marissa thought, wondering what it was. There was no way to apologize without asking what she'd said that had made him uncomfortable. "That's all any of us can do. Do you have any idea what time you'll be home?"

Ordinarily he would, but not with the meetings in progress. He shook his head, then realized that she wasn't just making idle conversation before he left. "You have class tonight, don't you?"

She nodded. Digging into her pocket, she pulled out a folded piece of yellow lined paper. "I made a copy for you." It was a duplicate of the schedule she'd put on the refrigerator. He frowned as he looked it at. "Don't worry. If you're late getting home, call. I'll get someone to cover for me."

One day into the arrangement and he was already reneging on his word. She probably thought it was a sign of things to come. "In your class, or with Andrea?"

She didn't want to start out on the wrong foot and make him think that she was being cavalier. "I know an excellent baby-sitter," she assured him. "She had a great model when she was growing up."

"You?"

Dimples winked. "You guessed."

He glanced down at the paper she'd handed him. Her class began at six-thirty. "I'll be back in time." He'd make a point of it. He wasn't the only one making a presentation to the group. He'd see to it that he went first.

Marissa nodded. Was it her imagination, or did he look uneasy? "Great."

She was standing too close. Memories of bygone days shimmered in his mind. For one small moment he suddenly had the urge to kiss her goodbye, the way he'd always done when he'd left Christine.

But she wasn't Christine. And he wasn't the man he'd been then, either. Not for a long time now.

Picking up his briefcase, he shoved the paper she'd given him into his pocket. "I'll see you tonight." He didn't wait for her to say goodbye.

Marissa stared at the closed door. Now what was all that about? One second, she could have sworn he looked as if he was going to kiss her, the next, he was leaving, abruptly slamming the door behind him as if he thought she was going to follow him all the way to work.

Mr. Alec Beckett was not an easy man to understand. Shrugging, Marissa returned to the kitchen. She had a lot to do before he came walking through that door again.

Chapter Seven

Alec was determined not to be late. He'd set his alarm for seven, an ungodly hour to be getting up on a Sunday, but those were the breaks when you were helping to nurture a fledgling software company that paid you a sinful amount of money for the use of your brain. They figured that the body just went along with it, like a matched set.

His body would have rather remained in bed, but there was no way around going out today. With a sigh, he got up.

He had to admit that up until now, they had been pretty flexible for him. It seemed only fair to repay the favor when they asked. And this hectic schedule *was* only temporary.

Besides, now he had help he could rely on.

With Marissa in his life, Alec thought, turning the shower on high, things had really fallen into place. She'd come in and had everything organized within a day, just like a benevolent drill sergeant—with curves. Had to be her army background.

Whatever it was, he was grateful for it. Looking back,

Alec had absolutely no idea how he had managed all this time without her. Here only a little more than a week—a week and a half to be exact—and she had everything running as if there was a Swiss watchmaker behind each separate component.

Andrea was thriving, he had hot meals on the table, and there was someone waiting for him when he got home at night, someone who made intelligent conversation. Albeit, three nights the conversation had been abbreviated because she had to get to her classes, but a little bit of something good was better than a huge slice of nothing at all. Or worse, complaints. Ellen, the last nanny, always had a litany of grievances to go over as soon as he walked through the door. This was like a piece of heaven.

He did feel slightly guilty because, so far, he hadn't been able to live up to his side of the bargain. He'd had to go into the office every day this week and hadn't been able to help out on Wednesday as promised.

Undaunted, Marissa had taken both Andrea and Christopher to the college day-care center with her. He had tried to make amends by paying for Christopher as well as Andrea, but he still felt that he owed her one.

One? Hell, he owed her a lot more than one, he amended, stepping out of the shower. He grabbed a towel and quickly passed it over his body. For the way she was making everything run so smoothly, he'd probably be in debt to her for the rest of his life.

Don't get carried away, he warned the wet, bedraggled reflection in the bathroom mirror. It didn't pay to get caught up in things. You get caught up, carried away, and then, one morning you wake up and there's no foundation under you, so you go plummeting down to earth with a resounding crash.

Alec didn't intend on being slam-dunked twice in his

life. He was a fast study and once was more than enough for him to learn his lesson.

Hurrying into his clothes, he blow-dried his hair and then ran a comb through it. He needed a haircut, he thought, looking into the mirror. Something else to put on the ever-growing list he never got a chance to fully deplete.

Absently, he wondered if Marissa cut hair. She seemed to be able to do just about everything else with a certain amount of flair. What kind of a jerk had her ex been, letting a woman like that go?

If she was *his* wife—

His thoughts abruptly halted. She wasn't his wife, she was Andrea's nanny and that was all she was. All she was going to be. He couldn't allow the lines to get blurred just because of one slightly sensual dream.

Slightly sensual. Yeah, right. Just like Phoenix was slightly hot in the middle of summer.

He had to exercise better control over his thoughts than that, or he was going to wind up regretting it.

As he made his way down the stairs, he became aware of music. A jazzy little number that pulsed through him. Exercise music, he thought, recognizing Marissa's tastes. Judging from the source, Marissa and company were in the family room.

The beat and the accompanying sound of childish laughter guided him into the room. He stopped just short of the doorway.

Marissa was on the floor with the children. That was nothing new. Alec hazarded a guess that she was probably on the floor with the children almost as much as she was upright. As he surmised, she was doing exercises. But these, she was doing alone. The children were only watching. He didn't blame them. She was wearing leggings and a leotard instead of her customary baggy, comfortable shirt.

The outfit she had on now might also make her comfortable, but it was having the exact opposite effect on him. The dark green leotard hugged every curve, every dip of her body as she twisted and turned, moving as effortlessly and supplely as a spring breeze.

Fascinated, he remained where he was, forgetting that he was supposed to be on his way to somewhere else.

She wasn't wearing a bra, he realized as Marissa stretched and bent backward, her head touching the floor just above her feet. The material stretched along the firm, athletic body, making him warm. He roused himself.

How the hell could she bend that far? he marveled. He'd break in two if he tried something like that. It hurt him just to look at her.

It hurt him just to look at her, he thought again, the words playing along his mind, this time with a completely different meaning.

He wasn't aware that he sighed, but she was. Surprised, she turned in his direction.

Marissa flushed, rising. "I didn't realize I had an audience."

"I was just leaving." But he wasn't. He was just standing. And staring. Suddenly aware that he was, he cleared his throat. "How do you do that?"

"With lots of practice." Marissa picked up a towel and dried off the sheen of perspiration at her neck. He was dressed as if he was going to the office. For a man who was supposed to work out of his house, he certainly wasn't in it very much. "That's a little formal for breakfast, isn't it?"

"I'm on my way out. To an unofficial meeting," he clarified. There was a long, thin dark stain that ran down the front of her leotard. He couldn't take his eyes off it. Off her.

Marissa draped the towel over the back of her neck, holding on to the ends. She looked at him in surprise. "You work on Sundays, too?"

Guilt nibbled at him. He hadn't spent nearly enough time with Andrea this week. He'd even had to skip the Baby and Me classes. He knew Andrea wasn't old enough to mind, but he was, and did. "Not usually."

Marissa hadn't been here long enough to know about "usually." It seemed to her that the man was almost married to his job. That wasn't healthy for anyone, especially not his daughter.

But it wasn't her place to lecture. Still, she couldn't help nudging his conscience along just a little. "I thought you told me that you worked at home a few days a week."

He knew what he'd said and knew that it seemed as if he'd lied. He hadn't meant things to go this way, but it was out of his hands. Things would get back to normal again soon. In the meantime, she'd have to bear with him.

"I do. Just, it seems, not this week."

Alec watched as she bent to pick up Andrea before the little girl crashed into the coffee table. Murmuring something into her ear, Marissa placed her in the playpen. Andrea began gnawing on her plastic blocks.

"You, too, young man." Marissa scooped up her son and placed him next to Andrea. Christopher began gathering blocks together, ready to duplicate his escape trick. But the blocks were plastic, not wooden, and flattened beneath his feet. "Gotcha," Marissa laughed.

Frustrated, Christopher tried again as Andrea looked on. The two children, much to Marissa's relief, were getting along beautifully.

Alec joined her beside the playpen. "I can't tell you how grateful I am that you're here." His train of thought almost disappeared as she turned to look at him. The effect her eyes had on him grew rather than diminished with familiarity. "I really don't know what I would have done without you." The words seemed to dribble out of his mouth slowly. He cleared his throat and tried again. "I promise that I'll make it up to you when I get back."

Marissa shrugged. She smoothed down one lapel that was turned slightly. Her fingers lightly brushed against his chest. Beneath the fabric, he felt rock solid. "There's nothing to make up. I'm the nanny. I'm supposed to be watching Andrea."

He had to concentrate to form words. Why did standing close to her cause every last drop of moisture to evaporate from his mouth? "But I also agreed to work around your schedule, not you around mine."

She smiled, her eyes crinkling. "Yes, I vaguely remember that was the deal."

Maybe it was the coward's way out, but it was his only option. He took a step back, away from her. "And you've done much more than any nanny could. I can't believe you've only been here a week."

"That's because it's a week and a half."

He inclined his head, accepting the correction. "See, you keep better track of things than I can. I swear, Marissa, if I didn't know any better, I'd say you were a godsend."

"You can say it," she said as she turned her attention to their surroundings. "I don't mind." She'd finish exercising later, when he was gone. Right now, the family room was a veritable obstacle course, littered with toys. Marissa began picking them up and chucking the toys into the huge box in the middle of the room. There were enough things here to stock a toy store, she thought.

He knew he should get going, but he couldn't seem to make himself. The woman didn't have an ounce of fat to spare, he thought as he admired the view.

Something distant and needy stirred within him. He pushed it away, upbraiding himself for behaving like an adolescent in heat. He was grateful she couldn't read minds.

"All right," he laughed. "You are. A wonderful god-send, dispatched just in time to deliver me from the brink of total and complete collapse and to keep me from going insane."

She turned around and raised her eyes to his. There was amusement in them. As well as something else. A knowing look. Maybe she could read minds, at that, he thought, suddenly uncomfortable.

Her smile took him prisoner. "With a testimonial like that, maybe I should ask for a raise." She deposited several more toys into the already overflowing box.

Marissa was worth twice the salary they had initially agreed upon. He'd be the first to admit that. "If you want to renegotiate—"

She was only kidding. The salary he was paying her was more than she had expected. It wasn't money now, but time that she needed.

"I'll settle for some free time to work on my paper tonight." She hesitated, then added, "And a crack at your computer if you don't mind." She had planned on renting one to type the final copy of her paper, but it would be nice to have one at her disposal while her thesis was still in the rough stage.

Computers were so much a part of his life, he sometimes forgot that not everyone owned one.

"Feel free." Alec paused. Was he going to insult her if he offered to give her pointers? "You know how to use one?"

He looked as if he was afraid he was going to hurt her feelings. That was sweet, as well as unexpected. The man had his moments, she thought.

"Yes, I just can't afford one right now. The cost of diapers and baby food keep eating into the money I was putting aside to buy a computer."

There was an old one in the office he could probably get

for her. A little tinkering on his part and he could have it up to speed, ready to compete with the current models in no time.

He really should be going, he reminded himself. He'd promised to meet with one of the potential backers and Rex by ten for brunch at the Sheridan in Newport Beach. Orange juice, bagels and lox, and software. It made for an interesting combination.

Though he knew that he should already be in the driveway, getting into his car, Alec couldn't seem to make himself take more than a couple of steps. And they were toward her, not the door. "Nothing fazes you, does it?"

If he was referring to the fact that she couldn't afford to buy what she considered luxuries because she had to spend it on someone very precious, it was no contest.

Marissa straightened a pile of computer magazines Alec had left on the coffee table and the children had subsequently tried to eat. "Lots of things faze me," she admitted. "I just don't let them stop me, that's all." Her eyes held his for a moment. "If you let any one thing overwhelm you, then it's won and you've lost."

He stooped to retrieve a magazine that had found its way under the table. Alec placed it on top of the stack. "Is that how you see life, in terms of win or lose?"

"Sometimes." She aligned the magazine on top of the others. "But it's not black and white, that's for sure. And every bad thing usually has something good come out of it."

He laughed dryly. "Now that sounds like something you'd find inside a fortune cookie."

She took no offense, sensing none was intended. "I adore fortune cookies."

That gave him an idea. He was serious about wanting to make this up to her. It had to be damn inconvenient. She hadn't had a day off since she'd started. "How about Chinese food?"

She wasn't sure what he was asking and didn't want to make a mistake by jumping to a conclusion. "It goes with the cookie."

He took that to be a yes. "Okay. Tonight. On me."

Marissa stopped fixing cushions. "Are you bringing it home, taking me to it, or wearing it?"

He laughed. Since she'd been here, he found himself laughing more and more. And feeling good. He knew the danger in that and tried to distance himself, but it was impossible. So impossible that he was beginning to stop trying. Everything was short-lived, he rationalized, so he might as well enjoy it while it was happening. It would be over soon enough.

Good things usually were.

"Your choice," he offered.

It had been forever since she had been to a real restaurant, but that would necessitate getting a baby-sitter, one who could handle two children. Both Jane and her mother were unavailable tonight. That narrowed her options.

"Well, as tempting as seeing you decked out in moo goo gai pan is, getting the stains out would probably be hell. And going out won't work, so, by process of elimination, I guess you're bringing it home."

It would be best that way. No misunderstandings. And yet he couldn't help wondering why she didn't want to go out. Was she afraid to go out with him?

"Why won't going out work?"

There was something in the way he looked at her, something that made her forget to breathe. Sometimes, she actually forgot how really handsome he was, until he looked at her like that and she remembered all over again.

She shrugged, feeling a little awkward. "Because we can't get a sitter on such short notice."

He wanted to take her out. To be alone with her in a crowd. He knew he was on dangerous ground here, but he couldn't help walking. "Your friend—"

"Is busy," Marissa said with genuine regret. "And so is her mother. I can't get anyone else on such short notice." There was his mother, but she wasn't going to suggest that. And since he didn't, she knew that he was just making a gesture. A very nice gesture, but a gesture nonetheless. "Besides, you don't really want to take me out."

How the hell had she arrived at that conclusion? "I don't? Why don't I?"

"Because you're busy. Because..." Why was she explaining this to him? Didn't he know? Or... "Do you?" she asked in a surprised whisper.

Yes, he realized, he did. He wanted to take her out. Not to show his appreciation for the way she was handling every rough spot in his life at home, but because she was Marissa. Because her hair smelled like wildflowers. Because he'd dreamed of her again.

He was standing so close to her, she could almost taste him. Her throat felt like parchment left out in the desert sun. She could physically feel the seconds ticking away as her body poised, waiting. Waiting for that final contact.

If he stayed here one more minute, he was going to do something he'd regret.

Something he wanted to do.

"I'd better go." But instead of leaving, he slid his hands along her shoulders slowly, thinking of the soft body that was just beneath the thin material. He stood there as if he'd been frozen for all time on a frame of film.

She could feel her body begin to hum like a tuning fork that had been struck. "Alec?"

He liked the way his name sounded on her lips. He wondered if it tasted as sweet as it sounded. "Yes?"

She said the words before her courage flagged. "It won't hurt anything if you kiss me."

He could feel his body aching. Why wasn't he leaving? Running? While he still had the chance...

Who was he kidding? He had no chance at all. "I don't know about that."

They were destined to kiss, she knew it, felt it. More than anything, she wanted him to be the one to make the first move.

"Aren't you the least bit curious?" Her voice was low, husky, part innocence, part temptation.

Curious? Hell, if he were honest, he'd thought of nothing else. It kept sneaking up on him, trying to break through the smoke screen he'd thrown up. The one meant to smother all his feelings, except the ones he'd consciously allowed to flourish for Andrea.

His fingers tightened on her shoulders. "You know what they said about curiosity and the cat."

She wanted this, she thought. Really, really wanted this. "Last I looked, neither one of us was a cat."

His hands slipped from her shoulders, down along her arms and rested on the swell of her hips. Her answer amused him, even as her presence stoked a fire long thought extinguished. "Aren't you supposed to be practicing child psychology?"

There was a smile in her eyes if not on her lips. "There's a little bit of child within all of us."

He couldn't draw his eyes away from her mouth, the way it moved when she spoke, the way it curved as she smiled, not at him but into him. He could feel the indelible mark of her smile within his breast.

It was a silly, hopelessly romantic thought, and he had long since stopped being a romantic. Maybe he was just suffering from battle fatigue. He'd been overworked, over-stressed for a long time now.

Or maybe, just maybe, with his life filled to overflowing with Andrea and work, he was lonely and he needed to reach out to someone.

To her.

Alec didn't want to analyze what he was feeling anymore. Not with her body so close to his. It was enough that he did feel. He thought he'd forgotten how.

His heart pounding madly in his ears, Alec lowered his mouth to hers. The last thing Alec heard, or thought he heard, was Marissa whispering, ''Geronimo.''

He had to be hallucinating.

A moment later he was convinced of it. It was all a hallucination, what she said, what she did. How he felt. Because he knew that kissing a woman couldn't feel like this. Had never been like this. He felt as if he'd just voluntarily stood in front of a mule and asked to be kicked in his gut.

That was the kind of wallop her kiss packed.

Stripping him of his breath, his mind and probably his very identity, she sent him reeling to the edge of space. To the edge of a black hole that had never been entered before. He probably wouldn't return alive.

He deepened the kiss and went in.

Everything within Marissa sang as she felt the hard imprint of Alec's body against hers. She wrapped her arms around his neck and leaned further into him, into the kiss that was drawing out every single thought she'd ever had and leaving her in a state of complete disorientation.

She'd known it.

Known from the very start, in her heart, if not in her mind, that it would be like this. That his kiss could have this effect on her. It made the very ground tremble beneath her and yet it filled her with such peace that it almost brought tears to her eyes.

Bells. He heard damn bells ringing. Just what did this

diminutive woman pack into her kiss? Struggling for release, Alec pulled his mouth from hers with a ragged breath. The ringing continued.

"I think it's the telephone," she whispered, unable to speak any louder. Not without being able to breathe.

For a moment Alec could only stare at her mutely, dumbstruck. He liked being prepared for things. There was no way on earth he could have been prepared for this. Nothing to tell him that every one of his defenses would be incinerated by the merest touch of her mouth.

Damn, but he wanted to kiss her again. To make love with her in his bed.

In the bed where he had made love with Christine.

The thought came crashing down on him, amputating the joy that had begun to sprout within him at its source. He couldn't go through this again.

Alec heard his own voice as the answering machine picked up.

"Hi, this is Alec Beckett. I'm unable to get to the phone right now—"

To get to the phone? Hell, he was unable to get to a coherent thought right now. But the sound of Rex's disembodied voice had a sobering effect on him. That, and the thought of what he'd almost allowed himself to do.

"Alec, I hope you haven't left because I lost your damn mobile phone number and I can't reach you any other way. The brunch has been pushed forward to nine-thirty. I need you with those charts *now*."

Like a man in a trance, Alec walked over to the answering machine and pushed the speaker button. He didn't feel as if he had the strength to lift the receiver. "Hello?"

"Alec? Is that you? What's the matter? You sound strange. Are you sick?"

His eyes were on Marissa. She looked as shaken as he

did. It didn't make him feel any better. "No. No, I don't think so."

Alec was looking at her as if she'd just stepped off the mother ship and asked to be taken to his leader. Why? Hadn't he enjoyed what had just happened here? She had. Infinitely. And it had nothing to do with the fact that she hadn't been with another man since Antonio had walked out on her. She hadn't wanted to be with another man.

Until just now.

Marissa drew in a shaky breath and dragged her hand through her hair. He looked upset, she thought. She didn't want him to be upset. She wanted him to be happy. She was. But men, she remembered, were easily frightened by what they couldn't control and she didn't think that either one of them could easily control what had just happened between them.

"Look, I want you to get here as soon as you can," Rex was saying. Alec was trying hard to concentrate on the sound of his voice and not the way his pulse was beating. "Maxwell is still undecided whether or not to throw his money into the deal and we need that money in order to go national. If anyone can convince him, it's you."

Right now, he didn't feel as if he could convince a rabbit to eat carrots. He couldn't think straight, let alone negotiate. Maybe his brain would defog by the time he got there. He fervently hoped so.

"Sure," Alec muttered. "I'll be right there."

"You sure you're all right?"

Alec hung up without answering the question. Not *knowing* the answer to the question. He didn't feel all right. And yet he felt wonderful. That was just the trouble.

He searched for the right words. She couldn't think that this meant anything. "Marissa—"

She knew panic when she saw it. Was he afraid she was going to ask for some sort of a commitment just because he'd kissed her and most likely branded her for life? She knew better than that. But she didn't want to hear him say anything to ruin the moment. "You'd better get going. That sounded important."

He looked at the telephone as if it was going to get up and walk away at any second. "It was—is. Look, what just happened here—"

"Was very nice," she said a bit to quickly, "but it shouldn't make you late."

Was it all right? Was he the only one affected? "What should it do?"

To say anything at all would be premature. But to deny that it ever happened was wrong, too. "I haven't figured that out yet."

There was nothing to figure out. It happened and it was over. "Marissa, I'm not looking to buy into anything."

Did he think she was laying a trap for him? She didn't know whether to be angry or hurt. She was a little of both. "Good, because I'm not selling anything," she said with a cheerfulness she didn't feel. "Now, I suggest you get to your brunch."

"Right." He leaned over the playpen and kissed Andrea, then eased his tie out of her hands. She was as fast as he was slow, he thought. Stepping away from the playpen, he straightened his tie. "I'll be back as soon as I can," he promised without looking at Marissa. He hurried out of the room.

"Alec," Marissa called after him.

He stopped without turning around, braced, waiting. "Yes?"

She came up to him, then handed him his briefcase. He'd left it in the hall. "You forgot this."

He stared at the briefcase for a minute as if he didn't know what it was. He certainly didn't know who he was anymore, he thought. "Oh. Yes. Thank you."

God, he sounded like a robot, he thought. Or an idiot. He wanted to stay here, to talk to her. To tell her that this had nowhere to go. And then to kiss her until she was as senseless as he was.

But Rex and Maxwell were waiting, so he did neither. Instead, he left. Walking out as fast as he could.

Chapter Eight

The hours, comprised of minutes that were dipped in molasses and mounted on the backs of snails, were dragging on. It reminded Alec of days he'd spent in boarding school, when he was trapped in a classroom, waiting for the bell to ring, proclaiming him free.

He was finding it hard not to fidget and wondered how long he should wait before sneaking another look at his watch. He'd already made his pitch and answered Maxwell's myriad of questions, all, apparently, to the man's satisfaction. Now they were just listening to the man talk. And talk. And talk.

There was no doubt that the man was entertaining, but Alec didn't want to be entertained. He wanted to be home. With Andrea, he added, afraid that even in the confines of his own mind, he had to keep vigilant watch over his thoughts. Ever since he had kissed Marissa, his mind hadn't been his own to command.

Maybe this would only go on a little bit longer. It sounded as if Maxwell was almost at the end of his story.

So far, the brunch had gone very well. Rex, Alec noticed, was actually smiling instead of wearing that perpetually dour, worried expression that had become his signature. Rex was the money man behind the company. It was, he often said, his job to worry.

He didn't look worried anymore. It looked as if they finally had themselves a wealthy backer. About time, Alec thought.

"I like putting my money where it'll grow," Maxwell was saying as a coda to his story.

It seemed that there had been a point to it, after all, Alec thought.

Bruce Maxwell, a man with features that belonged on the face of a gargoyle and the disposition of a cherub, leaned back and patted the cigars in his jacket pocket. He looked down at them longingly. There were no sections set aside in the restaurant for smoking.

"A fine cigar'll seal this bargain." He slanted a mischievously sly glance at Rex. "That, and my check, of course."

Both men laughed. Rex's was a nervous one. Alec knew he wouldn't relax until the check had cleared, and not completely even then. Alec doubted that Rex knew how to completely relax.

Maxwell placed his large hands against the table and pushed himself away. "What say we leave before they pass some ordinance against smoking in a parking lot?"

Alec didn't have to be asked twice. He was on his feet even before Maxwell was. At last. Alec had begun to think that the brunch was never going to be over. Ordinarily, he enjoyed talking about his work. In their own way, his designs, his programs, were just as much a part of him as Andrea was. They were his creation, his children, and he wanted to assure their futures so that, ultimately, he could assure her future. Nothing was more important to him than Andrea.

But right now his mind wasn't on the future. It was on the past. The very immediate past. And a pair of lips that had seared their imprint into his very soul, marking him as surely as if a branding iron had been applied. Nothing that happened here in the restaurant, monumental though it was for the company and for him, even began to dim that effect.

Maxwell clamped a hand on Alec's shoulder in a gesture of camaraderie. Rex was bringing up the rear, having stopped to sign for the meal. He caught up to them at the door. Maxwell waited until they were all out, well clear of the entrance before he produced three cigars, each wrapped in cellophane.

It reminded Alec of Native Americans passing around the peace pipe after a council. In a way, he supposed it might be fitting, seeing as how Maxwell, who hailed from Arizona, was one quarter Navajo on his mother's side and fiercely proud of it.

Rex pocketed his charge card and accepted the cigar, looking at it a little uncertainly.

Maxwell turned toward Alec. "You smoke, boy?" At sixty-three and a millionaire several times over, Maxwell felt entitled to call any man who appeared the least bit younger than him "boy." Because of his friendly manner, and habit of freely spreading money around, no one took offense.

Alec felt Rex eyeing him. In a potential state of misery, Rex undoubtedly wanted company. Friendship had its limits. Alec had no desire to feel his brunch repositioning itself in his stomach. Shaking his head, he declined the offered cigar. "No, I don't."

Maxwell pressed the cigar into his hand anyway. "Then just smell it." He ran his own slowly under his nose and inhaled deeply, like a man on the threshold of ecstasy.

"The subtle scent tempts." Taking off the cellophane, he looked at Alec. "Like a fresh-faced woman giving you the eye. It's not an experience to be rushed into, but savored."

Like kissing Marissa.

Alec pushed the thought from his mind. A kiss was a kiss and that was the end of it. Especially since he was never going to make that mistake again.

Maxwell bit off the tip, then slowly inhaled the cigar's dormant aroma again before he lit it. He raised a brow to Rex.

The latter mimicked him, removing the tip and then presenting the cigar to him to be lit. Rex did his best not to appear as miserable as he felt. One of them had to join Maxwell in this ritual.

Under normal circumstances, Alec would have gladly hung around to see if Rex actually turned green. He'd known Rex for ten years now, ever since he and Joe Forrester had formed Bytes and Pieces, and in all that time, he had never seen Rex take so much as a single puff of anything.

It would have been interesting to watch him now, but he was anxious to leave. "You won't be needing me anymore?" The question was addressed to both Rex and Maxwell.

Rex looked uncertain. His background wasn't nearly as technically oriented as Alec's was. And he did lack some of the man's enthusiasm when it came to the actual programs.

But Maxwell waved Alec on his way. "No, I'm through with questions for today. Go on home to her, boy."

He hadn't said anything about Andrea to the man. How did he know? "Her?"

The bewildered look on Alec's face only made Maxwell laugh. "There's a woman on your mind, boy. Nothing makes a man fidget like a woman. I'm old. I know the signs. Don't think I haven't seen you sneaking peeks at your watch. Go on home to her," he repeated, grinning.

He saw Rex eyeing him curiously. Rex's wife, Myra, had already tried, unsuccessfully, to lure him over for dinner twice with the sole intention of fixing him up with one of her single friends. He'd turned the invitation down both times.

"There is a woman," Alex admitted. "Or a woman in training, actually. She's a year old," he explained when Maxwell raised one thick gray eyebrow. "My daughter Andrea."

Maxwell shook his head, not about to accept Alec's denial. "No." He puffed slowly, watching a ring rise lazily into the air from his lips. "That ain't the one who's got you itchy to get going. I can see it in your eyes." Shifting his attention back to the smoke rings, he allowed the subject to drop.

Alec frowned. The man was talking nonsense. Cigar smoke had obviously gotten into Maxwell's eyes. He just wanted to get home to his daughter, that was all. He'd spent too much time away from her this week. He shook Maxwell's hand. "Nice doing business with you, Mr. Maxwell."

"Same here." He clamped his teeth around the cigar, shaking Alec's hand with both of his. "I'll be seeing you, boy."

Alec nodded at the men, backing away. He could see his car from here. It was parked several aisles over. Getting out would be a lot easier than getting in. The lot had emptied since he'd arrived.

"I'll see you at the office tomorrow," Rex called after him.

Alec turned around. "I was hoping to work out of the house tomorrow. I've got some catching up to do." On several fronts.

With Maxwell's backing, production was going to go into high gear. He needed Alec's input. "Half a day," Rex promised. "We'll split the difference."

Better than nothing, Alec supposed. "Which half?"

Maxwell nudged Rex. "Take the bigger one. Ask for morning." Mornings had a habit of bleeding into the afternoon, taking a chunk out of it before anyone knew it was happening.

"Morning," Alec reluctantly agreed.

He was happy for Rex, happy for himself, as well, he insisted. It looked as if they were about to play hardball with the big guys at last. Every large company, Rex was fond of saying, had been a small one once. And they had been small long enough. This was what he had been working toward all along.

So why wasn't he happier about it? Why was there this nameless, antsy feeling waltzing through him? Because he couldn't understand it, he dismissed it. He had a daughter to get home to.

He glanced at his watch as he got in behind the wheel. Two o'clock. Four and a half hours to wine and dine the man. But at least the rest of the day was his. He could finally go home.

But first, he had to make one stop on the way.

Both children had been even more energetic than usual. Marissa was grateful for the diversion. If she was busy, she couldn't think and if she couldn't think, she couldn't dwell on this morning.

The hell she couldn't. It kept popping up, fresh in her mind, like toast in a defective toaster slot that refused to stay down no matter how hard you pressed the lever. It hounded her throughout cleanup and all the little games she had played with the kids. It refused to let her have any peace, replaying itself over and over again in her mind.

Each time she relived it, her breath would back up in her lungs, and her pulse would race, just as it had when he had kissed her. When she ran her tongue along her lips, she could still taste him.

If only he hadn't seemed as if he'd wanted to break and run when he had backed away. But then, it had probably frightened him as much as it had her.

"The way to face up to your fears," she said aloud to the two children, "is to meet them head-on. I only hope your daddy knows that," she told Andrea.

Marissa looked up at the sound of the doorbell. Alec hadn't told her that he was expecting anyone. And it couldn't be him, unless he'd forgotten his key.

Picking up each child one at a time, she deposited them into the playpen. "You stay put, you hear?" she said over her shoulder as she went to the door.

"S'ay puu," Christopher echoed behind her.

"Right, stay put," Marissa agreed. "The legendary peephole," she murmured to herself at the door. Remembering her promise, she looked through it. There was a well-dressed, somewhat impatient-looking woman standing on the other side of the door. The doorbell rang again. Marissa winced as the sound cut right through her. She opened the door before the woman had another chance to press the bell. "Yes?"

The lady, a stately looking woman with hair the color of muted flame, slowly took measure of her. Her eyes, a vivid green, looked as if they missed nothing.

"May I help you?" Marissa asked.

The woman swept past her, royalty entering commoner grounds. "Is Alec in?"

"No, I'm afraid he's out."

The woman turned around. A smile faintly whispered along her lips. "Just as well. Then we can get acquainted without interruption."

Marissa noted a resemblance around the eyes and the set of the mouth. This had to be Roberta.

It was turning out to be one hell of an emotionally wrought day. First Alec scrambled her brain, then his mother arrived to pick over it. If she survived this, she could survive anything. "Mrs. Beckett?"

Roberta was obviously pleased at being recognized. "How did you know?"

"You have his eyes."

"He has mine."

Marissa conceded the point. "He has yours. Right this way, please," Trying to make the best of it, Marissa led the way into the family room. Andrea and Christopher sounded as if they were engaged in a tug of war.

When it rained...

Alec recognized the car as he turned onto his street. A vivid blue Mercedes sedan. It was parked, slightly askew, in his driveway.

Roberta.

She could never park worth a damn. What was she doing here? It wasn't her habit to just come by for a visit. If she wanted to see him, she summoned him. Like a queen commanding an audience.

Was there something wrong with Andrea?

It wasn't until he had parked his car and was hurrying to the front door that he remembered Marissa didn't have his mother's number. There was no way she would have called Roberta if she couldn't reach him.

So why was Roberta here?

Alec wasn't sure what he was expecting when he walked in. Probably Marissa's suitcases, packed and standing in the hallway. Roberta had that effect on women. She made them want to flee. Anyone younger than she was, was instantly the enemy, to be vanquished one way or the other. And

Roberta had a rapier tongue that was more than equal to the job.

Prepared for anything, Alec entered the house, looking around. The sound of childish babble and womanly voices led him to the family room.

He held his breath.

Marissa had mercifully changed from the body-hugging outfit she'd had on previously into shorts and a T-shirt. Not much of an improvement, he thought, but some.

To his amazement, Marissa looked completely at ease. Maybe Roberta hadn't had time to go for the jugular yet.

"Hello, Roberta. What are you doing here?" Walking in, he picked up his daughter and gave her a hug before setting her down on the floor again.

"Well, there you finally are," Roberta said, as if he were a delinquent nine-year-old who had been due home hours ago. "Is that any way to greet your mother?"

Alec saw the amused look in Marissa's eyes. She was amused rather than intimidated. His admiration for her grew.

"Sorry, I was just surprised to see you. And as for where I was, I was working, Roberta." Dutifully, he brushed a kiss on the cheek she presented to him. Her kiss was bestowed on the air beside his cheek.

Nothing changed, he thought.

"On a Sunday?" She narrowed her eyes in disapproval. "Isn't there something written about resting on Sunday?" She looked at Marissa for confirmation.

Marissa merely raised her shoulders and let them drop again. There was no way she was getting in the middle of this.

Alec caught the gesture and wondered what was going on. Were the two women actually getting along? Seeing as how one of the women was his mother, it didn't seem possible. Roberta didn't get along with women, she tolerated them. Sometimes.

He perched on the edge of the sofa arm, alert for the first signs of attack. Marissa would be no match for her once Roberta got rolling.

"Not if you have a rich backer to please."

"And did you succeed?" Marissa spoke for the first time.

He looked relieved to be addressing her instead of his mother, she thought. "Rex is actually smiling."

By the way he said it, Marissa took it to mean that this was not the norm for Rex. Whoever that was. She wondered if Alec was aware of the fact that he had left out a great many details about his job. She had only the sketchiest idea what he actually did. He wasn't free with information.

His mother, on the other hand, had been, whether she realized it or not. The short visit had filled in several gaps for her. The picture of a man who had been raised to believe that there was no such thing as love was beginning to emerge. That was why seeing him with his daughter was particularly touching. He loved his daughter. And he'd loved his wife. Marissa only had to hear him mention her name to know that.

Alec turned his attention to his mother. He still had no idea what she was doing here. "What does bring you out, Roberta?"

Long, dark lashes swept along the hauntingly high cheekbones that had cost her a fortune to attain. She studied her nails for a moment before answering. Roberta didn't believe in polite smoke screens. "I came to see if the woman you hired measured up."

Oh, God. "Roberta..." Alec began warningly.

Roberta ignored him, as she had done for most of his life. "I told Melissa here—"

"Marissa," he corrected before Marissa had the opportunity.

Roberta inclined her head, accepting the correction, and continued. "That men don't know how to conduct proper interviews. All they want is help. It's up to us women to see if certain standards are met."

Since when? Alec crossed his arms in front of him, looking down at his mother. What was she up to? "I thought your only standard was that the nanny be breathing."

"Don't be droll, Alec. You haven't the talent for it." She tossed her head, tilting her chin up, knowing that was her most flattering pose. She splayed her hand dramatically over her Armani-covered breast. "Just because I was never Carol Brandy—"

"Brady," Alec put in.

"Doesn't mean that I don't care about Andrea." Her eyes shifted toward Marissa. "I wanted to find out just what sort of a person you had hired to take care of her."

He didn't know whether to be embarrassed or just plain angry at this intrusion. Roberta had picked a hell of a time to play grandmother.

"Roberta," Alex began, his voice tight, "could I see you for a minute?"

Roberta made no effort to get up. "You see me now, dear."

His eyes narrowed. He had no idea what kind of game Roberta thought she had in mind, but Marissa wasn't about to play it. "I mean, in private."

"Later." She waved him away, looking at Marissa. "When I'm through."

He could see the way she was sizing Marissa up. She was no match for his mother. No woman was. He had to find a way to get Roberta to sheath her claws before they sliced Marissa. Alec had no intentions of standing by and seeing her hurt.

"Why the sudden interest, Roberta?" he pressed in an attempt to divert her attention to him. "You never conducted impromptu interrogations before."

"Interviews, darling, not interrogations. I do wish you'd use your words properly. And before, the nannies you hired always came through agencies that screened them properly. That's not the case now, is it? This is a tedious job, I grant you, but someone has to do it." She sighed, indicating that she would bear up to the burden. "We were almost finished when you arrived." She turned toward Marissa. "Just a few more questions, if you please."

Okay, maybe this wasn't so bad after all, Alec reasoned. Marissa looked none the worse for it. Maybe he was worrying needlessly.

"Have you ever been arrested?"

Alec shot to his feet. Boy, when he was wrong, he was really wrong. "Roberta!"

This time, it was Marissa who raised her hand to silence him. She could take care of herself, although she had to admit that having Alec come to her defense was rather touching. She couldn't remember the last time something like that had happened.

Marissa's eyes were on Roberta's. She gave no indication that she was going to look away. Or be intimidated. "No."

Roberta purposefully looked at Christopher. "Have you ever been married?"

"Roberta, I don't think—"

"Yes." Marissa's voice was calm.

Roberta took in a long breath before asking, "What happened?"

"Roberta, you've gone too far," Alec said sharply. "That is none of your business."

Roberta looked appalled that her son should speak to her that way, or that he thought that anything was beyond her right to know. "Of course it is. What if he left her because she was abusive?"

For almost thirty years she'd hardly bothered with him and she had to pick now to try out for the role of Donna Reed. "You're being ridiculous." Alec looked at Marissa, praying that Roberta hadn't insulted her enough to make her want to leave. "Marissa, I'm sorry about this—"

Marissa's eyes darkened, not at the question, but at the memory. "My husband left because he didn't want a child. Because he couldn't share his heart with someone small and helpless." She pressed her lips together, looking at Christopher. If Antonio had had his way, Christopher would have never been born. And the best part of her would have never existed. "Someone who needed him."

Intrigued, perhaps even moved though she'd be the last to admit it, Roberta looked into Marissa's eyes. Her expression was unfathomable as she studied the younger woman. "But you can."

There was no hesitation, no doubt in her mind. Marissa raised her chin. There were a lot of unknowns in her life, but this wasn't one of them. "Easily."

Roberta nodded, rising. She'd heard enough. Stayed long enough. "She'll do," Roberta informed Alec as she left the room.

He stared after his mother, stunned. She was walking toward the front door. Leaving. He had expected something long and drawn out, a scene in which he would be forced to come to Marissa's rescue.

Quick and painful, that was his mother's modus operandi.

Alec hurried after Roberta. He caught her arm, turning his mother around to face him. "That's it?"

She looked at his hand until he disengaged himself. "That's more than enough." She patted his cheek. "She'll be fine for our girl."

If he didn't know any better, Alec would have said that he detected a trace of envy in his mother's eyes. As if she were jealous of Marissa. Not of her looks, but of something else.

But that wasn't possible. Roberta didn't envy anyone. She expected to be envied.

"'Our girl,' Roberta?" he repeated. Since when had she really had a hand in helping with Andrea, other than the few times he had all but begged her to watch his daughter while he worked?

"Of course." Roberta laughed at his incredulous tone, choosing to see no basis for it. "You bring her to me whenever you need help, don't you?" She shook her head, making eye contact with Marissa who remained in the other room. "They forget when they need us."

Alec was speechless. When had this happened? When had Roberta suddenly joined forces with Marissa? As far back as he could remember, his mother had never regarded any woman equal enough to share a sentiment with. She considered herself as someone who resided on a higher plateau than other women.

Sighing, Roberta took her keys out of her purse. "Well, I'm off. Scott Baron is taking me to the races." She placed one hand delicately on Alec's arm, sharing a confidence. "It's a dreadful bore, really, but I do like eating in the boxed seats." She rolled her eyes heavenward. "They have the most fantastic chef."

Dropping her hand, she looked at Marissa again. Obeying the silent summons, Marissa came forward, Andrea in her arms. Roberta lightly passed her hand over the child's head, barely making contact. "Take care of them," she instructed Marissa.

Marissa smiled. She had every intention of doing that. It wasn't in her to do things by half measures. "Yes, ma'am."

Roberta cringed, but to Alec's amazement, she didn't chastise Marissa. "Roberta, please. 'Ma'am' makes it sound as if I'm old."

"Never happen, Roberta," Alec muttered mechanically. He looked pointedly at Marissa and saw that she understood. He wanted to be alone with his mother before she left.

"Nice meeting you," Marissa told the other woman, withdrawing. Andrea curled against her, sucking her thumb, ready for her.

"Lovely girl," Roberta commented.

Something was definitely up. Roberta never handed out compliments. Even under duress. "All right, Roberta, what's this all about?"

She looked at him innocently. "It's about your well-being, dear. Yours and Andrea's. Weren't you paying attention? I was conducting an interview for you."

It wasn't an interview, she was satisfying her curiosity. Why couldn't she just admit to it? "You were checking her out."

Her look silently asked him what his point was. "Same thing."

He laughed and shook his head. Not by a long shot. "Not where you're concerned."

Roberta raised one elegant shoulder in a familiar gesture that he unconsciously repeated time and again. "Maybe I was just interested in the new woman in your life." She looked at Marissa's retreating back as the latter went up the stairs, both children in tow. "You haven't seen anyone since Christine died."

Whoa. This was coming out of left field. "I'm not seeing anyone now, Roberta, except in the strictest sense of the word. As in, with my eyes open." She laughed at his protest, as if he were a small boy to be humored. He hated it when she did that.

"Whatever you say, dear. But I beg to differ. If you really believe that, then your eyes aren't open at all." The smile was a regal one. "I do approve. Of her," she added since he looked as if he didn't understand what she was saying.

Not that it would make any difference to him if she didn't, but he was curious. "Why? You don't usually approve of any woman."

"That's not true. It's just that I have standards, Alec. Very high standards." For a moment she seemed to soften right before his eyes. "Just as you do." She smiled at him. "I do care, you know. In my own fashion, I care. About both of you."

It made him uneasy, seeing her like this. Was there something wrong? "Is there something you want to tell me, Roberta?"

"No, nothing," she replied lightly, rousing herself. The soft look was gone. "Well, take care, darling." She brushed another kiss into the air above his cheek.

Alec stared after her disappearing figure, completely bewildered. Was she just being Roberta, or had there been an actual attempt at communication just now?

As usual, when it came to his mother, he didn't have a clue.

Chapter Nine

When he walked back into the house, Marissa was just coming down the stairs. To Alec's relief, she still didn't look upset. If anything, she appeared to be amused by his mother's visit. How she could be still escaped him. Any other woman would have taken offense at Roberta's questions. He was beginning to think that Marissa was a rare human being.

He was waiting for her to say something, Marissa thought, to get him off tenterhooks. "Your mother's very colorful."

Alec followed her into the family room. Marissa began straightening up. Needing to do something with his hands, he joined her. The place looked as if a hurricane had hit it. He supposed, in a way, it had. Hurricane Roberta.

"She's something, all right." He threw a cushion back into position, then looked at her. He couldn't quite decide if Roberta had left her unfazed or if Marissa was just very good at hiding her feelings. "I'm sorry if she insulted you."

It hadn't occurred to her to be insulted. She didn't think that had been the woman's intention. Marissa collected a handful of blocks from the coffee table, holding them against her. Christopher had left his mark everywhere and his mobility was tempting Andrea, urging her to try to catch up. Marissa had no doubt that within a few weeks, they would both be flying around this room and things would be twice as chaotic.

"She was only worried about you. And Andrea." Marissa didn't think he realized that.

"Worried? Roberta?" He hooted at the notion. That would be giving her credit for having traits like a mother and Roberta had never been one of those except by biological definition. "The only thing she ever worries about is whether or not she can continue to look like a glamorous woman in her early thirties."

He didn't even know how old his mother really was. The one time he'd asked her, years ago, she had evaded the question by saying he didn't need to know that. He knew for a fact that she changed the year of her birth each time she had to fill out a form that required the information.

He'd been hurt, Marissa thought. A great deal. The first woman he had ever turned to in his life had rebuffed him. It was bound to leave some sort of scars. How could a mother *be* like that?

Marissa ached to soothe him.

If only he'd let her.

"She's doing a great job," Marissa answered lightly. She got down on her knees to scoop up a pile of colorful puzzle pieces around the perimeter of the coffee table. A couple had teeth marks in it. "She looks more like your sister than your mother."

Alec dropped the puzzle board on the floor and joined her, fitting the wooden pieces in one at a time. A barnyard scene began to emerge. He'd seen Marissa sitting with the children, patiently enunciating the name of each animal and then guiding chubby fingers until they found the right place for the piece. *She* was a mother, he thought. Not Roberta.

"She'll be happy to hear that. It's the look she's going for." Finished, Alec put the wooden puzzle aside. "How bad did it get?"

"You were here for the worst of it," she assured him. "Don't worry about it. Your mother's a piker when compared to the Sergeant."

"The Sergeant?" That was almost as bad as having to call his mother Roberta. "Is that your father?"

"Was," she corrected. She placed Andrea's lop-eared bunny in the playpen. "He died a few years ago. A casualty in one of those peace-keeping missions that are so awfully misnamed."

When she'd mentioned her father earlier, Alec had no idea that he had died. "I'm sorry."

"Don't be. It was the way he would have wanted to go. In a foreign land, on duty for his country." That was his first love, she thought. The service. He would have been a lot better off if he had never swerved from his dedication and had that fateful tryst with her mother. Her mother would have been better off, too. "My mother remarried the following year. First time I ever saw her happy."

"Was he hard on you, the Sergeant?" He tried to imagine what it must have been like for her, growing up with a strict military man for a father. He wondered if that was better than not having a father at all.

She shrugged. Time had a way of softening the edges, taking some of the pain away. She understood her father better now, knew that he'd done the best he could, given his temperament.

"He didn't think so, but, yes, he was. Harder on me than the others because I was the oldest." And she was to be an example to the others. "Because I had no buffer the way they had."

She had been their buffer, he thought. She was like that, protecting the weaker ones. A bantam rooster, dancing around the cock of the walk to divert his attention.

Marissa retrieved a half-eaten cookie from behind the television set, wondering how it had gotten there. "Every time I got home from a date, it was like a scene right out of *Marathon Man*. You know, where Laurence Olivier is asking Dustin Hoffman questions. Except that the Sergeant didn't know how to pull teeth. At least—" she laughed quietly, it was a sad sound "—not literally."

What had she been like as a young girl? he wondered. "Did you go through that a lot?"

There was no nostalgia when she thought of those days, only relief that they were behind her. "No, fortunately, the Sergeant was away a great deal of the time. I guess he thought he had to make up for it when he was around." She was making excuses for him, but it was easier to believe that than to think he had done it to satisfy a set of principles. "Most fathers do it with quality time and family outings, mine did it by making sure we were growing up the way he wanted us to." She lifted her chin, her shoulders back, standing the way her father always demanded that she stand when he lectured her. She could almost hear his voice ringing in her ears as she repeated, "'Straight and upstanding. Honorable. Good solid citizens.'" She looked at Alec, letting her body relax. "Old habits are hard to break. But it did do wonders for my posture."

She was making light of it. Was it because she was embarrassed at this glimpse she was giving him into her past, or because of her unflagging good humor?

"You sounded as if you were reciting that."

"I was. It was the Sergeant's credo. After all these years,

I know it by heart." She sighed, shrugging. "What little he allowed me to keep."

Alec sincerely doubted that anyone could take away her spirit. "I get the feeling that no one 'allows' you anything, Marissa." He had the urge to touch her, to kiss her again and feel what he had this morning. He forced himself to keep his hands in his pockets. "You do what you want to."

His assessment amused her. More than that, it pleased her. "Is that what you think?"

He turned, taking Andrea's huge not-so-white teddy bear and placing it on top of the toy chest. "That's what I think."

Marissa nudged him aside and lifted the lid. The teddy bear leaned precariously back against the wall as she deposited one last toy into the box. She let the lid drop into place again.

"You might be half right." She straightened and looked up at him. "I don't overstep any boundaries. But in here—" she touched his chest "—and here—" she feathered her fingers along his temple "—I'm my own person. No one tells me how to think, how to feel. That was always my business."

Why was it, no matter where he moved within the room, he always seemed to wind up like this, standing beside her? Close to her. He looked down into her eyes. Was she putting him on notice?

Or did he just want her to?

As her hand slid away from his face, he caught it, slipping his hand over it. Alec closed his fingers around Marissa's and just held her. As firmly as her eyes held his.

"Like I said, you're very independent," Alec whispered, inclining his head toward hers so slowly that he hardly seemed to be doing it at all. Until his lips were almost on hers. "I never thought of independence as being sexy before."

It was happening again. The ground was liquefying beneath her feet and she was standing on nothing, waiting to free-fall through space. "And now?"

"And now—" his breath warmed her "—I do."

Alec couldn't stop himself, no more than a bird could keep from flying. He thought he could, but he couldn't. Her kiss had lingered on his mind throughout the entire four-and-a-half-hour meeting. Throughout the drive to the office and then home. Haunted him until there was nothing else on his mind but her.

He *had* to see if the magnitude of his reaction was just because he hadn't kissed a woman since Christine had died. Since his soul had died. Maybe his mind was playing tricks on him, taking a tiny seedling and turning it into an entire symphony of flowers just because the field was so totally barren.

And ripe for fruition.

That had to be the reason that just one taste had been enough to form such an impossibly romantic reaction within him.

He had to find out. He had to kiss her again. If he was rationalizing, so be it. But he had to know, no matter what the cost.

Alec's mouth covered hers. Instantly the kiss deepened, whether by his design or hers, he wasn't sure. He just knew it had. And he was falling in.

His hands cupped the back of her head. He wasn't bringing her to him as much as trying desperately to anchor himself to something that still existed in the real world. Because she was sending him off again, off to regions that were so far beyond his scope of knowledge they sucked away his mind, and then his will.

He was hers. For this one moment he was hers completely, body and soul. Because he hadn't romanticized his reaction to her. If anything, he'd downplayed it.

She did nothing with the gift. Nothing, save to give him something in return. She gave him herself. He could feel it, taste it. There was surrender in her kiss, surrender aligned beside the power.

He wanted more.

She gave him more.

This time, Marissa didn't hold back. This time, she wasn't stunned. She was prepared. Prepared to lose herself, to savor, to enjoy reaping the unexpected harvest thrust into her possession.

She could feel everything, hear everything. Music, the sound of his ragged breathing. Her own blood pumping madly through her veins. She was a part of it all. One with it.

And yet, there was nothing else in the world, but him. Only him.

Alec.

She wondered if he knew what he was doing to her. If he understood what was happening. Marissa wasn't all that sure that she did. But she knew she wanted it to go on forever.

Marissa wrapped her arms tightly around his neck, moaning from the sheer pleasure that flowed through her body. Pleasure that he created.

Slowly, Alec pulled away, shaken, concerned. Bewildered. For a moment he framed the side of her face with one hand, just looking at her. Into her eyes. Looking at the woman who had almost unwound him like a spool of runaway thread.

What the hell was happening to him?

He swallowed, trying to get his bearings. It wasn't easy when his compass was missing. "I didn't want to do that."

She read his eyes and had her answer. "Yes, you did."

He didn't know why he couldn't seem to control himself, but she had to know that there was no future in this. That he couldn't let her think this would lead to anything but awkwardness. Just as it was doing now.

"Marissa—"

"Shh." She laid a finger to his lips. He wasn't ready for this. She understood. But she didn't want to hear him deny his feelings, either. "No apologies, no regrets." She searched his eyes, looking to see if some part of him understood. "It happened. Twice. And it was lovely each time. That doesn't mean you have to marry me. Or that you're being unfaithful." Something flickered within his eyes.

Though he didn't seem to move a muscle, she could feel him stiffening. As if she'd hit a nerve. "Why would you say that?"

She could see through him, she thought. Even without his mother's input. "Because you're the kind of straight arrow the Sergeant would have approved of. A man who gives his heart just once and believes it's gone forever." His brow rose. "Your mother gave me some background on you." That didn't sit well with him, she could see it. "I didn't ask, she volunteered."

That didn't sound like his mother at all. Alec released Marissa, placing more distance between them. "She did?"

He didn't look as if he believed her, she realized. That bothered her a great deal. "She did."

Maybe Roberta was changing. He wouldn't have thought she would stop by to pay a visit, but she had. Maybe this was part of the new Roberta, too. In which case he'd better be forewarned. "What exactly did she tell you?"

"The truth," she answered simply. "That you hadn't been out since...Andrea was born," Marissa concluded tactfully, thinking his daughter's birth was a better way to mark time than his wife's death.

Roberta had no business thinking she could just barge into his life like that, not after keeping out of it for almost thirty years. His eyes narrowed as he looked at Marissa. "And how would you know if that was the truth?"

That answer was simple. "Because you don't kiss like a man who makes a habit of getting around."

"And you're an expert on that?"

She forgave him the trace of sarcasm, even though it stung. "I haven't been out with anyone myself since before Christopher was born. At first, it was because I was pregnant, and then I didn't see the point."

"The point?"

"I wasn't looking to get involved with anyone, so why go out?" Marissa grinned. "It wasn't exactly as if I had time to kill."

This was making him nervous, she thought, the kiss and what was behind it. Well, he wasn't the only one. But her nerves had more to do with a sense of anticipation, his seemed were the result of something akin to dread. That, too, she could see in his eyes.

The moment needed to be lightened. Marissa stepped away. With the children down for a nap, she had time to herself. If there was such a thing, she thought. What with a new routine to get down for the class and wrestling with a thesis that refused to assume a proper form, time to herself meant time to do her own work. She'd forgotten what it was like just to read a book for its own sake, one that didn't have a philosophy, or fuzzy animals that talked.

Marissa looked at him, suddenly remembering what he'd said when he left. "So, where is it?"

"It?" he repeated, bewildered. He thought she'd been talking about them.

No, he corrected himself. There was no them, there was just a kiss, nothing else. He couldn't allow there to be anything else. What he was feeling was delayed remorse, that was all. But he couldn't just seek solace with the first attractive woman he was physically drawn to. It wouldn't be fair to either of them. At the very least, it would lead to complications, and that was the last thing he needed now. He didn't want to care about anyone else besides Andrea. He didn't want the pain that was involved in caring. Not ever again.

They were wrong. It wasn't better to have loved and lost. It was hell.

"Yes, 'it.' Chinese food. You promised to bribe me, remember?" A smile played along her lips. "I guess not. You forgot."

He had. Chagrined, Alec knew there was no way to talk his way out of the oversight. After four and a half hours in the restaurant, take-out food had been the last thing on his mind.

Alec spread his hands. "Completely. Guilty as charged."

She didn't need the extra salt anyway. "Just as well. One of us might get a suggestive fortune cookie." She winked at him.

"But I did bring you something."

She turned around, surprised. What could he have possibly brought her? "Oh?"

He saw the interest in her eyes immediately. It made him think of what she must have been like as a little girl. He wondered if anyone had thought to give her things then. It didn't sound as if either one of her parents had doted on her the way he did Andrea. Or loved her.

He knew how that felt. It wasn't until Christine that he even knew love could exist.

"It's in the car," he told her. She began to follow him. "You stay here. Better yet, this is going to take me a while. Why don't you go do something?"

"Want me to start dinner?"

"No, not dinner." He couldn't even begin to think of food. "I still owe you that. Find something else to do."

He didn't owe her anything, but it was nice that he thought so. "You're being awfully mysterious about this."

Yes, he was, Alec realized. And he was enjoying himself. Enjoying the look of anticipation in her eyes.

"I know." He grinned.

Marissa shook her head as he disappeared from the room. Alec Beckett was one difficult man to figure out. One moment he was pulling her toward him, the next, trying to set up roadblocks. And then the process began all over again.

He certainly was different from Antonio. Everything with him had been up front. What he wanted. What he didn't want. There were no real surprises after the first few days. She'd known from the start what he was all about. She'd just hoped that somehow, what he was could be altered just a little. That love would make him want to alter.

Clothing was altered, she reminded herself. Not people. She'd learned that lesson just a little too late to do her any good.

"Sure I can't help?" she asked. Alec was almost at the front door.

He only stopped long enough to tell her, "Yes, by staying out of my way."

He'd aroused her curiosity. And her. She only hoped that for him, this attraction between them was a good thing. She already knew that it was for her. She'd thought herself emotionally comatose, if not dead altogether. She had Alec to thank for making her discover that she could still feel. It was a nice thing to find out after all these months.

It took Alec less time than he thought. Setting up the old computer had only taken a few minutes. What he had assumed would take longer was upgrading the CPU so that it could run faster for her. He'd picked up the part at a computer store on his way home after stopping at the office.

But even that had gone fairly routinely. So had installing

her screen saver, the one he'd created especially for her. Twenty minutes later, he went looking for her, anticipating the expression on her face when he told her that the computer was hers to keep. Rex was only going to get rid of it and use the write-off for the company. Now that Maxwell was aboard, there was no need.

He found Marissa in the family room. She was on her stomach on the floor, trying to retrieve a small stuffed animal that was wedged somewhere behind the breakfront in the half inch of space that existed between it and the wall.

For a second he watched as she wiggled and angled for position. Entertained, he squatted behind her, addressing the back of her head.

"If you're trying to crawl behind that, there's not enough space."

Marissa started, scraping the inside of her arm along the back of the breakfront. She'd been so intent on reaching the stuffed animal, she hadn't realized he'd come into the room. Marissa winced as the scrape began to sting.

"Very funny. Andrea flung her rabbit behind this when your mother was over. I'm just trying to get it out for her."

He tried not to stare at her butt, even though her shorts adhered to it invitingly. "Leave it. She'll never miss it. And if she does, I'll buy her another one."

Must be nice, she thought, not having to worry about money. There had never been a time when she hadn't worried about it.

"If you say so." Marissa tried to snake her way out again. It wasn't as easy as getting in. It wasn't easy at all. "Um, Alec, would you mind giving me a tug?"

His eyes traveled up the length of her. "Which part would you like me to tug?" He could think of a number of places he wouldn't mind wrapping his arms around.

"You can start on my other arm." She wiggled her fingers. "I seem to be stuck."

She was serious, he realized. "Hang on, I'll get you out." But as he tried to move the breakfront back further, he found that it was too heavy to maneuver without help.

"Okay, we're going to have to do this the hard way." Wrapping his arms around her waist, he pulled, at first gently, then harder.

The last tug did it. They tumbled backward on the floor, a tangle of bodies, arms and legs. Her breath whooshed out of her as she landed on top of him.

It wasn't an unpleasant turn of events, Alec mused. Looking up into her face, Alec ran his hands along her sides slowly. He could feel her, every inch of her, against him. His body hummed in response. It had been a long, long time since he'd felt like this.

He smiled into her face, brushing the hair away from her eyes. For a moment temptation urged him on. It would be so easy to give in. So very easy. His fingers curled along her cheek, touching it softly. "I don't think we'd better start something we can't finish."

She braced herself above him, a host of sensations scrambling through her like a mass of electrical impulses.

"No," she agreed slowly. "Until we can both finish it." *And it won't be today.*

With a sigh, she rose, first to her knees, then to her feet. Venus, rising, he thought, not from the sea, but from an idiot who couldn't take his opportunities where he found them.

But he wasn't that kind of a man. Even if he were, she wasn't that kind of a woman. He knew that instinctively.

Marissa brushed herself off, rotating her shoulder. She looked at the scrape on her arm. "Thanks for the rescue."

Taking hold of her arm, he examined the scrape. "Did you just do that?"

She nodded. She tried to pull her arm away, but he wouldn't release it. "I'll live."

"You better put something on it." Then, before she could protest, he took her by the hand and led her into the bathroom. Opening the medicine cabinet, he took out the disinfectant. "Hold out your arm," he instructed.

"You've been watching too many medical shows." But she did as he told her.

"Better safe than sorry." Lightly, he brushed the applicator along her scrape. "A one-armed nanny leaves something to be desired."

"I suppose so." It hardly stung. "You have a nice touch."

"So they tell me." He grinned. "Better?"

"Better." She dropped her hand at her side. "Thank you."

"Don't mention it." He liked doing things for her, he thought. It gave him a good feeling. "Ready to see what I brought?"

She placed her hand in his. "Ready." She still hadn't a clue as to what he could have possibly brought her, but whatever it was, she was prepared to love it.

Alec led her to the spare bedroom, where he had stored his old desk. He'd intended to call the Salvation Army to come and pick it up, but somehow or other, he'd just never gotten around to it. He was glad now he hadn't. It was perfect for the computer.

"There." Standing in the doorway, he gestured toward the computer.

It didn't look like his computer, but then, she'd only seen it once in passing. "You set up your computer for me in the spare bedroom?"

He pulled her into the room. "Not my computer. Your computer."

"Mine?" She circled it, not sure what he was telling her. The computer was turned on. As she looked at it, she realized the screen saver was a photograph of Christopher.

Before her eyes it transformed into an image of her. Stunned, she looked at Alec.

Her reaction pleased him. "Just a little trick."

She watched, fascinated, as the image turned back into her son. "I don't understand. Are you lending me a computer?"

"No, I'm not lending you a computer, I'm giving you a computer."

Much as she wanted one, it was out of the question. "I can't accept something like this. It's too expensive."

"Once, yes," he agreed. "This is an old one from the office. No one uses it anymore. We got in a shipment of replacements a month ago, the last word in technology. This one's antiquated by current standards, but I've upgraded it enough so that it'll more than suit your needs."

Her eyes were as wide as a child's at Christmas. He didn't think he'd ever forget the way she looked right now. "And you're giving it to me?"

"Yes."

She couldn't quite make herself believe that he would have gone to all this trouble for her. No one else ever had. "For my thesis."

"And for anything else you need. It's yours, Marissa." She looked as if she didn't quite comprehend what he was telling her. As if something was keeping her from believing him. He pulled the chair out for her, silently urging her to sit down at the desk. "Hasn't anyone ever given you anything before?"

She shook her head. Marissa sat like someone just waking from a dream.

"No," she whispered. She looked up at him, her blue eyes shimmering through newly formed tears. "I don't know what to say."

"Then don't say anything." Her gratitude made him uncomfortable. It was only a computer. A secondhand one at that. "Just type." He indicated the keyboard and began to back away. "I've got to run out for some Chinese food."

She looked at the screen and watched her son's face being formed out of her features. Alec had done this for her. Taken time away from a schedule that was as crammed as hers to create something to please her. There were no words she could offer him that began to say what she felt.

The sound at the door roused her. He was leaving. "Alec?"

"Yes?"

"Thank you."

Alec didn't answer. He merely waved his hand at the sentiment as he walked quickly out. Her gratitude undid him even more than her kiss had.

Chapter Ten

"Alec, you have to come."

Alec frowned as he repositioned the telephone receiver between his shoulder and his ear. Sunday brunch was one thing, having to spend an entire evening socializing when he'd much rather be at home was another.

"Rex, I have to create programs that'll sell, that'll entice the public to spend their hard-earned money and clamor for more. I have to help you continue to build the company's reputation for excellent software. I don't *have* to attend a party."

"You do if I'm giving it for Maxwell. How will it look if my chief creative guy isn't there?"

Behind him, in the kitchen, Alec could hear Marissa talking to one of the children, coaxing them to eat. His dinner was getting cold, he thought. He didn't feel like having this conversation, especially since he had a sneaking suspicion he wasn't going to win. "Almost ten years in the business, two degrees, and suddenly I'm reduced to a 'creative guy'? What kind of a technical term is that?"

Rex's deep voice echoed in the receiver as he laughed. "It's what Maxwell calls you and if it's good enough for him..." The rest went unsaid. "C'mon, Alec. You can even wear a disguise. It's a costume party."

Alec stifled a groan. "Costume party. Oh, this is just getting better and better all the time." Grown men and women, reliving their childhood by running around in Halloween outfits. It was something he could definitely do without.

Rex ignored the sarcasm. "And if you don't have anyone to bring with you, Myra has this friend..."

Alec closed his eyes. Could this get any worse? He didn't care for social gatherings that included more than three people, hated dressing up in outlandish clothes, and dreaded being "fixed up." Why married people were so obsessed with coupling their single friends was beyond his understanding.

Moving the telephone, Alec turned around so he could see what was going on in the kitchen. Marissa was ably handling both children. So what else was new? She made it look so easy. Whenever she left him with both children in the evening, they wore him out before the first hour was up.

Rex was making lofty plans in his ear. He knew if he didn't say something, he was going to wind up sitting beside Myra's friend at dinner. "Now I have to bring someone?"

"No, aren't you listening? I said, Myra has this friend—"

He'd seen some of Myra's friends. "I'll bring somebody," Alec promised quickly.

Victorious, Rex knew the value of a quick exit from the field of battle. "Great. I'll tell Myra you're coming. That's Saturday. Eight sharp."

"You'd better hope I don't bring anything sharp," Alec

muttered, hanging up the receiver. He sighed, shaking his head as he walked back into the kitchen.

"Problem?" Marissa looked up from the spill she was cleaning. Andrea thought carrots looked better on the floor than in her dish.

"No. Yeah." He looked down at his place mat. It was empty. Had she cleared off the table already? He knew she was in a hurry, but he wasn't even half finished with his dinner.

Marissa looked amused at his ambivalence. "Multiple choice?"

"Rex wants me to come to a party." He looked around and didn't see his plate in the sink. "Marissa, where's my dinner?"

"Right here." She opened the microwave. "I was keeping it warm for you, in case the conversation ran over." Marissa set the plate back in front of him. "It sounds like fun. The party, I mean."

His dinner was warm. And she was incredible. "You like parties?"

She sat down again between the two high chairs. Christopher was fussing a lot tonight; she hoped he wasn't coming down with something. "It's been a long time, but, yes, if memory serves me, I like parties." Marissa coaxed the small, pink lips apart with the edge of the spoon. "Just a little more, sweetie." Christopher clamped down on the spoon and sucked.

She glanced at her watch. She had forty minutes before she had to get to class. That left her just enough time to finish feeding the children, throw something into her own mouth, put the dishes into the dishwasher and leave. Life was really becoming way too scheduled these days. She wanted to leave pockets of time for surprises, but there weren't any pockets available.

There weren't any more surprises lately, either, she reminded herself. After a month of being here, things had settled into a fast-paced routine. The magic she'd felt between her and Alec was still there, but he was doing his best to ignore it and she couldn't very well force him to acknowledge its existence. It always took two.

Still, she couldn't complain. Life was better now than it had ever been before. And there were all these wonderful possibilities looming on the horizon for her. Not the least of which was that she was going to have her degree in less than a month. That would open up a whole host of doors for her.

She had to be content with that.

Content. It was an odd word to settle for. Once she would have been thrilled to death to reach her goal. But now that it was within her grasp, it felt a tad empty. She wanted something else. She wanted more.

That was her problem, she thought disparagingly. She always wanted what she couldn't have. And she couldn't have him, couldn't have the complete life she secretly yearned for. Not until he wanted it, too.

Dinner tasted great, even after being reheated. But Alec's mind wasn't on his meal, good as it was. It was on Marissa.

Big surprise.

No matter how hard he tried, how well he tried not to do anything stupid to perpetuate a situation he had no business being in, he couldn't seem to exercise that same control over his mind. It was almost as if the more he tried not to think about her, the more he did. What she said, what she did. He'd see her reading to the children, or teaching them how to roll a ball between them without eating it. And of course, there was class, when he could make it. She was always in class, moving, stretching, tantalizing without knowing it.

It was small wonder he couldn't do a good job of not thinking about her. There were traces of her everywhere in his life. And if she wasn't around, her cologne was. It lingered throughout the house.

He was never going to be able to look at flowers again without thinking of her.

Alec knew he should consider his words carefully, but this was just in self-defense against one of Myra's "fix-ups," nothing more. "Rex wants me to bring someone."

"A date?" There was no reason for her pulse to suddenly accelerate like this. Alec could see whoever he wanted to. She'd already convinced herself that even though he'd kissed her, it hadn't meant anything. At least, not to him.

The word date made him uncomfortable. He would have rather not thought of it that way. "For lack of a better term," he demurred. "Actually, he threatened me. He said Myra would have one of her unattached friends there."

Amusement lifted the corners of her mouth. "And that's a threat?"

It certainly was to him. "How do you feel about blind dates?"

She shrugged as she wiped Andrea's hands. The little girl had decided to wrestle her for the spoon and had gotten apple sauce all over her fingers in the process. "I don't know, I've never had one. Awkward, I'd imagine."

He looked at her incredulously. "You've never had a blind date?"

Why was he so surprised? "No. I always knew who I was going out with. Or thought I did," she murmured more to herself than to Alec. She'd known who she was going out with, she amended. She just hadn't known the depth to which his stripes ran. She hadn't known he was unshakably set in his ways.

"Well, they're awful, take it from me." He'd had a few arranged by well-meaning friends before Christine had entered his life. "You spend the entire time stumbling through six-word sentences and subtly trying to look at your watch, hoping the minute hand has suddenly taken on wings instead of being stuck in glue.''

"That does sounds pretty terrible," she agreed.

"It is." And if he didn't ask someone, he was going to allow himself to be sentenced to that sort of thing all evening.

Alec leaned back and studied Marissa. She was still feeding both of the kids, coaxing a spoonful of food into one, then using the downtime to do the same with the other. Even with all the things she had to do in her own life, she still managed to have the household running far better than anyone else who'd filled the position before her.

She made life comfortable for him, he thought. Maybe a little too comfortable. And yet, there was this edginess just outside the perimeter, waiting to come in, to claim him if he let it. An edginess that excited him even as it scared the hell out of him.

Was he making a mistake?

There was only one way to find out.

He picked his plate up and took it to the sink, buying himself a little time as he brushed the remains into the garbage pail.

"Marissa," he began slowly, "how would you like to rescue me?"

She wasn't going to hope, she told herself. He hadn't tried to kiss her since the Sunday he'd given her the computer. He didn't mean what she wanted him to mean. "You want me to call Rex and say that you can't come because you have a broken leg? Or been abducted by aliens?"

Setting the dish into the dishwasher, he shut the door, and then turned around to look at her. "All viable possibilities, but Rex would want proof in either case." He watched her face. "I was thinking more along the lines of you coming with me."

"To a party?"

"To a costume party."

He seemed to cringe as he said the word. She could think of nothing more exciting.

Well, actually, she could, but she'd tried not to let herself think about him very often, not in that light. Not when he was trying so hard to distance himself from her. It seemed as if giving her the computer was her consolation prize. He had taken himself out of the equation that night and left her on the outside, looking in.

Now, it seemed, the door was open again. Had he changed his mind? Did he finally recognize the needs that she had already seen within him?

She could feel the smile rising to her eyes. "I'd love to." A costume. She was going to need a costume. Something to blend with his. "What are you going as?"

The thought of having to wear a costume *really* made him not want to go at all. "I was thinking of going as a computer programmer."

Why was she not surprised? "You are a computer programmer."

Alec nodded. "I know. Makes finding the costume easy." He'd told her it was a costume party so that she could find one for herself and not feel awkward when they arrived. He had no intentions of wasting any time looking for something to wear himself.

If they were going, they were going to do it right. "Leave it to me," she promised, wiping Christopher's mouth. "I'll take care of everything. Now, I've got to get going before I'm late. The kids are all changed and fed. Bedtime's at seven-thirty. I'll see you later."

And she was gone.

Yup, he thought, taking Andrea out of the high chair and then reaching for Christopher, he'd just made a mistake. A big one.

So why did it feel so good?

* * *

"A pirate?" Alec stared at the open box on the sofa. He'd had to go in today for half a day. A half day that had turned into longer than a regular whole one. He was more than ready to forget about the party, except that Marissa had sounded so excited when he'd walked in. He hadn't seen her, but she'd called out to him and told him she'd be right out. His costume, she said, was in the family room.

"You want me to go as a pirate?"

"No, not a pirate, a Gypsy." He obviously hadn't looked at the outside of the box. "And not just any Gypsy. You're the Prince of the Gypsies."

As if that made it better, Alec thought, holding up the wide, fawn-colored breeches. Was she kidding? "I don't have to wear a crown, or tights, do I?"

She laughed. Was it her imagination, or did that sound incredibly sexy? "Only if you want to."

"I don't even want to go," he told her. He held up the shirt. The sleeves were wide enough to hide Andrea in. This was ridiculous. He wasn't going to wear something most women wouldn't be seen dead in. "I don't see why—"

He stopped as she walked into the room. The words dried on his lips, fading away. She looked like a Gypsy, all right. A Gypsy queen. Her slim hips were girdled with a multi-colored scarf that dipped wantonly on one side. Her white blouse was scooped at the bodice, showing off bare, creamy shoulders. The skirt was made of yards and yards of material that flowed around her like leaves dancing in the autumn wind.

"You don't see why what?" she coaxed when he didn't finish his sentence.

"I don't know." He stared at her, mesmerized. "I forgot."

Alec moved around her slowly, drinking her in, a sip at a time. She looked like a colorful whirlwind. A myriad of thin gold bracelets clinked at her wrists whenever she moved her hands while wide, gold hoops swung invitingly from her ears, drawing his attention to the slim column of her neck. Her hair curled around her, a dark storm of waves. It made him long to run his fingers through it.

His tongue felt like lead in his mouth. "God, but you are beautiful."

Marissa flushed, pleased. Eyes slanted to look more mysterious, Marissa ran her thumb over her fingers. "Cross my palm with gold, handsome sir, and I shall tell you what the future holds for you."

He already knew what the future could hold for him. If he were brave enough to risk it.

Alec picked up the box. "I'd better put this on," he murmured.

"And I'll put the children down for the night." For simplicity, Christopher was going to remain in Andrea's room tonight.

He nodded. "They ought to get a kick out of the costume." He smiled broadly. "God knows, I do."

Marissa left the room, smiling. "Hurry up, we don't want to be late."

"Yes, we do," he said over his shoulder as he went up the stairs to his room.

Rex had pulled out all the stops. He'd even hired valet parking for the evening. Smartly dressed attendants quickly approached arriving cars. Just how many people were coming tonight?

Alec handed his keys to one attendant as he got out. Another was holding the passenger door open for Marissa. He saw admiration in the man's eyes as he looked at her. Not that he could blame him, Alec thought, rounding the hood.

He took Marissa's arm and led her to the front entrance.

"I still don't understand. How did you manage to talk Roberta into staying with the children?"

Never in a million years would he have thought his mother would give up a Saturday night to do something so mundane as baby-sit her granddaughter.

"I take no credit," Marissa said innocently. "It was completely her idea. I was going to call Jane to baby-sit. All I did was mention the party to your mother when she called earlier. The rest is history."

Alec guided her up the steps. "Not my history," he assured Marissa. "I'm going to start looking for a pod in her basement. That woman who came over tonight is not my mother." There was something different about Roberta lately. Softer. As if she'd suddenly realized that she had allowed something precious to slip by all these years. What other explanation was there for her sudden interest in his life? It wasn't exactly maternal, but it was close.

"There are no basements in Southern California," she stated flatly.

"Just shows how tricky these aliens really are." Leaning past her, Alec rang the doorbell. His arm accidentally brushed against her breasts. He could feel a warmth creeping over him, reminding him of when he had pulled her free from the breakfront. How her body had felt against his.

He was making himself crazy. Because with the yearning came the fears, the memory of how bereft he'd felt after Christine had died. And how he had vowed never to feel that way again. The price for that had been isolation.

The price for feeling again was the promise of pain. He didn't want to go through that again. But he didn't want to relinquish what was happening, either.

"Sorry," he murmured.

"It's all right, it was an accident." Was she being wanton because she didn't want it to be an accident? Because she wanted him to want her?

A somewhat rounded Robin Hood opened the door, calling a halt to any further exchange.

Rex lifted the dark green mask away from his eyes, getting a better view. He recognized Alec immediately, though Alec knew his partner had half expected him to arrive in a suit.

"Alec?"

If Rex grinned any more, Alec thought, his face would split in two. Alec ushered Marissa into the tiled foyer. Music, mixed with the sounds of voices raised in conversation and laughter, was coming from the ballroom.

"It's me," he assured Rex. "Don't rub it in."

Rex was already turning his attention to Alec's companion, taking her hand in his and kissing it as befit the courtly era his costume represented.

"And this is?" He raised an inquiring brow toward Alec.

"Marissa." Alec slipped one arm around her shoulders. It was a purely proprietary move and he was ashamed of himself, but he made no attempt to remove his arm. "Marissa Rogers, this is Rex Wellington, part owner of Bytes and Pieces. And a former friend."

Marissa inclined her head. "I've heard a lot about you."

"And I have heard absolutely nothing about you." He looked at Alec accusingly. "Who is this beautiful creature?"

"I'm the nanny," Marissa explained simply, sparing Alec the trouble of going into details he'd rather leave unsaid.

"Myra," Rex called into the ballroom, even though there was no way his wife could hear him. "We have to get some children. Quick."

Marissa laughed. "Don't encourage him," Alec warned. Then, turning to Rex, he advised, "Get a hold of yourself, or Myra'll tighten her leash." Myra was a very jealous woman, though Rex had never given her any cause.

There was always a first time, Alec thought, seeing the way Rex was looking at Marissa.

"It might be worth it," Rex mused. "Come, I'll introduce you to everyone."

"I already know everyone," Alec attested.

"I wasn't talking to you." Rex hooked his arm through Marissa's, extracting her from Alec. "So, how long have you been nannying?" he asked as he pulled her into the ballroom.

Alec followed behind them, feeling the oddest sensation working its way throughout his body and centering in his chest. He would have said that he didn't have a jealous bone in his body. But if this wasn't jealousy, what the hell was it? He was feeling positively territorial about Marissa, and annoyed that Rex had taken her over.

There was absolutely no reason to feel this way. Rex was his friend, and married in the bargain. Happily married. And Marissa was her own person. He had no say in her life any more than she had one in his, beyond where it affected his daughter.

He plucked a goblet of wine from the tray of a passing waiter and resigned himself to making the best of it.

He had no say in her life beyond where it affected his life, Alec amended half an hour later. And seeing her in the center of a circle of men, laughing at something one of them was saying, was definitely affecting his life.

He'd put up with it long enough.

Alec placed his glass of wine down on the first available flat surface and excused himself from the woman who had been talking to him. At least, he thought it was a woman. It was someone dressed as a pink rabbit. The voice coming out of the rabbit's head was muffled and he really hadn't been listening to anything the rabbit had to say.

He'd been too busy watching Marissa. Telling himself that he didn't care how many men talked to her.

It was a lie. He did.

It was stupid on his part, but God help him, he did. He didn't want her talking to anyone but him.

Coming up behind her, Alec tapped Marissa on the shoulder. Was it his imagination, or had her blouse slipped a little since they'd walked in? He didn't remember her cleavage looking quite that ample, quite that tempting, before.

"Want to dance?" he asked when she turned toward him.

There wasn't a moment's hesitation. She was sure the others would excuse her. "I'd love to."

Someone else within the circle, a man dressed like George Washington, put his hand out to her. "Then why don't we—" he began.

"She's with me." Alec all but growled the words, taking a firm hold of her hand. He didn't say another word as he led her to the dance floor.

Marissa nestled against him, amusement in her eyes. "You're supposed to be a Gypsy prince, not a caveman."

He opened his mouth to defend himself and then closed it again. She was right. "Sorry, did that sound a little gruff?"

She nodded. "I was expecting you to drag me off by my hair any second. There was no need, you know. I had every intention of dancing with you." She leaned her head against his shoulder. "I was just waiting for you to ask me."

That same scent of wildflowers began filling his head. Worse than a drug, he thought. It was beginning to disorient him, make him think of things, want things. "You looked like you were having a good time."

She raised her head to look at him. "I am. Now."

"You looked like you were having one before."

She glanced over her shoulder, feeling a little like Cinderella at the ball. This was a wonderful change of pace from what she was accustomed to. "Your friends are nice. I like them."

He shrugged, trying to sound indifferent. "They're all right. What was he saying to you? Joe. You were laughing." He knew he was failing. He sounded as disinterested as a police detective investigating a homicide.

"Just a funny story." She looked at him closely. "Alec, are you jealous?"

He avoided her eyes, looking, instead, over her head at the small five-piece band Myra had hired. They were dressed like the early Beatles, with one to spare. "Why would I be jealous?"

They both knew he was behaving that way. "Because you seem rather annoyed that I was over there, talking to other men." She didn't want him thinking that he owned her just because she cared about him.

His hand tightened around her waist. "Maybe, since I asked you to the party, I thought that you'd be with me instead of..." He caught himself. What the hell had come over him? He was behaving like some mindless jerk. "I'm sorry, did that sound as hopelessly adolescent to you as it did to me?"

Tension gone, she smiled up at him, lighting up the room. "Yes, but that's all right. In a way, it was kind of cute."

Alec sighed, pressing her closed hand to his chest. "I don't know, whenever I'm around you, I just don't seem to think straight."

"You don't have a monopoly on that, you know," she told him softly.

He shouldn't feel this way. He knew where it would lead.

And yet, it was so good to be alive again. "So, what are we going to do about it?"

Was he really admitting that he felt something for her? Oh, Lord, she hoped so. "Take it one step at a time. That's all we can do."

No, that wasn't all. He could deny it. Deny it was happening. "Suppose I don't want to take those steps? Suppose I already know where they'll end up and I don't want to go there?"

She knew he wasn't talking about falling in love. He was talking about the consequences. The ones he'd suffered for loving his wife. But it didn't have to be that way.

"The interesting thing about a road, Alec, is that it can be widened, redirected, landscaped. You just never know until you go down it again just where it might actually lead."

She was making prophecies now. He grinned. "You're really getting into the part, aren't you?"

"Consider it a reading. On the house." She rested her cheek against his shoulder again and let the music take her away.

Whatever else happened, she had this moment and she was going to savor it.

Chapter Eleven

"It was a lovely party, wasn't it?" Marissa asked as she entered the living room. She had just finished checking on the children. Both were still asleep. She'd decided to leave Christopher in Andrea's room for the night, rather than take him back with her to their quarters. There was a baby monitor set up in her quarters that would alert her if either of the children was up and needed her. It was one of several units she'd had Alec purchase.

Roberta had left immediately after they'd arrived, declaring herself "too tired to talk." For all intents, they were alone.

It was late, time to call it a night. And yet he couldn't leave the room, couldn't take his eyes off Marissa as she walked toward him, her skirt swirling sensually around her legs with each step.

"Yes," he agreed, "it was nice."

She was surprised at the admission. "I think you actually mean that." It was a little thing, but it made her happy to know that he had enjoyed himself with her. Marissa stood in front of him, knowing she should be going, wanting to be exactly where she was. "What happened to the disgruntled Gypsy prince?"

"He became gruntled." Alec laughed. He was talking nonsense and enjoying it. Treading on quicksand again. How had that happened? "I guess I'm feeling a little intoxicated."

On one glass of wine? She sincerely doubted it. "I only saw you take one drink."

His eyes met hers and found themselves imprisoned. Alec rested his hands on her shoulders. "I wasn't talking about alcohol."

He held her so that her body was almost touching his. "Oh?"

"Yes, 'oh.'"

He slid his finger along the large hoop at her ear and with a slight tap, sent it swaying hypnotically. Everything about her was hypnotic. And if he wasn't careful, he was going to fall under her spell. As if he hadn't already.

"You do things to me, Marissa. Things I like. Things I don't think I should like."

The feeling was more than mutual. One look from him set off a tidal wave of emotion within her. "Why?"

He sighed, knowing he shouldn't hold her like this, knowing he was just making things worse down the line. But he couldn't help himself. Every time he was near her, he wanted her.

"Because if I do, I'll feel again." He was lying. He already was feeling things. Feeling things for her that scared him even as he ran to embrace the wild, exhilarating rush they created.

But then, he never did have much sense.

Marissa tilted her head up, searching his eyes, trying to understand what he was telling her. "And is that such a bad thing? To feel?"

"It is, for me." He traced his thumb slowly along her lower lip and felt desire grow within him. Saw it bloom in her eyes. "Marissa, I don't want to hurt you."

Ever so lightly, she pressed a kiss to his thumb. "You won't."

She sounded so confident. She didn't know, he thought, couldn't know. Her husband had left her, but their love had died before then. It wasn't ripped away suddenly without warning.

"I will," he insisted, his voice low. "Because I can't give you what you want. A home. A family. Stability." He knew the kind of woman she was, even though she had never made a single demand on him. He knew just by listening to her, by watching her. She had needs he couldn't fulfill.

She looked around the room. He already had a home and a family. She just wanted a small place within that. "I don't understand. You can't share this with me?"

It wasn't a place or a thing, it was larger than that. He could give her shelter, a house that went beyond anything she'd dreamed. But what she really wanted, he couldn't give her.

"I can't share me with you." It upset him to see the look in her eyes and to know he was responsible for it, but better a small hurt now than a much larger one later. "I'm a coward, Marissa. I've been there once. To hell." He said the words as if he were feeling the pain all over again. "It was all I could do to find my way back again. If it wasn't that I had Andrea to take care of, I wouldn't have made it." His eyes touched her face, hoping she could find it in her heart to forgive him. "I don't want to go to hell again."

Why did he have to pronounce what was between them dead before it ever had a chance to live? "No one's sending you there, Alec."

Christine hadn't expected to die, either. But things happened. And left behind shards of glass that slashed away pieces of a grieving heart. "But it's there, waiting for me. If—"

"If," she repeated. She knew what he was about to say. "If I should die." Marissa pressed her lips together, promising herself she wasn't going to cry. Tears weren't going to help. "Did I tell you longevity runs in my family? I have a great-aunt who's almost a hundred. And a few scattered relatives in their eighties." She took a deep breath. This wasn't about longevity, or dying. This was about fear. "You can't approach life just staring at a bottom line. The bottom line is there for all of us, eventually. But it's what we do before we reach it that counts." Her eyes pleaded with him to cross the line he'd drawn for himself. "I would rather have a little of something good than an eternity of nothing at all." She released a breath, searching his face for a sign that she had gotten through. "Does that make sense to you?"

He took her hands in his. She was a sweet, sweet woman and she deserved so much more than he could give her. She deserved someone who could love her unconditionally, without fear. That wasn't him.

"Logically, yes. Emotionally..."

She bit her lip. She'd meant it when she said she would take a little and be satisfied with it. "I'm not asking for commitments."

He knew better, even if she thought she was telling him the truth. His heart swelled at the sacrifice she was prepared to make. The one he couldn't allow her to make. "Your lips aren't. But your eyes are. You're not the sort of woman who would be satisfied with a casual affair."

Her eyes glinted like twin pools of warm, inviting water. "Try me."

He wished she would stop. He only had so much

strength, so much willpower. A man had his limits. "I won't do that to you."

She felt the tears begin to slip past her safeguards, wetting her lashes. Marissa drew herself up. "God, but you are noble." She backed away, trying to save a shred of her pride. She'd just thrown herself at a man and had him step aside, letting her fall. She felt as if she'd just crashed onto the concrete from a five-story drop. She had to leave now, before he saw her crying. "Well, I have an early day tomorrow." She turned away from him just in time. One tear slid down her cheek, paving a way for others. "So, if you'll excuse me."

She was walking away, leaving, taking temptation with her. It was going to be all right. All he had to do was retreat. Turn around and walk up the stairs to his bedroom.

He could tell by the set of her shoulders how much he had hurt her by refusing what she was so generously giving. Nobility warred with needs. It wasn't even close.

"Marissa?"

If he was going to tell her that this was for the best, she was going to hit him. This was hard enough to endure without being told that it was good for her. Because it wasn't. *He* was good for her. Alec made her happy, made her son happy. How could *not* being together be good for her?

Marissa barely had time to turn around before Alec swept her into his arms, his mouth coming down hard on hers. The passion he'd been trying so hard to deny captivated her, white hot and searing, instantly drawing a matching response from within her.

She tasted of tears, he thought. Tears he was responsible for. It was just the beginning, he knew, but he could no more stop himself than he could walk on water. It was beyond his control now.

Yes. Yes! Marissa wound her arms around him, wound

herself around him. She kissed him as if her very life had been given back to her.

Because it had.

His mouth raced along her face as Alec tugged at the edge of her blouse, pulling it out of the waistband of her skirt. He wanted to touch her, wanted to be with her in the wondrous, intimate way a man could be with a woman. The way he needed to be now, quickly, before common sense and his conscience caught up to him. Because everything he had said to her was true. He couldn't give her what she needed most, but he just couldn't help himself, either. This need for what she could give him was far too great.

He felt the blood rushing in his ears as he splayed his hands along her waist, holding her to him, worshipping her with his lips. Hungrily, he found his way back to her mouth. Over and over again, he kissed her, finding bits of himself within her offering.

Everything within her cried out for this moment. For at this moment, he was hers completely. She knew it was only a small window in time, but it was enough. It was all she needed to wedge in and find a place for herself within his heart.

She had needed this opportunity and now, suddenly, it was here in front of her.

And then, just as suddenly, it disappeared, chased away by the wail of a baby. By an urgent cry. Not any more urgent than what they were both feeling, but for the moment, at least, more important.

Marissa could almost feel her heart sinking within her breast. She knew if the passion stopped now, before it had time to bloom, before he could fully understand how much they truly did need each other, it might never begin again.

But they couldn't take one another when a child needed them.

"The baby," she whispered, her breath heavy against his cheek.

"Yours or mine?"

His brain swimming, Alec couldn't distinguish the difference between their cries. It was sheer agony to pull away from her, but he did. Andrea or Christopher needed her. And they were the ones who truly counted here, not this insistent burning within his loins.

Marissa dragged air into her lungs. It wasn't enough to still her racing pulse or silence the wild beating of her heart in her ears. She felt a sob rising in her throat and suppressed it.

"Yours." It was a pitiful, bleating sound that could mean anything. Most likely just a diaper that needed changing, but she had to be sure. Marissa was already backing away. "I'd better go see what she needs."

He could only nod, trying to pull himself together. "You'd better," he agreed quietly.

As she left the room, Alec sank down onto the sofa, rubbing his hand over his face, trying to gather his wits together. God, what had he almost gone and done? If Andrea hadn't cried out just then, he would have taken Marissa in the middle of his living room like some rutting animal, like some creature that couldn't think or use any self-control.

Just to satisfy his physical needs.

He wouldn't glorify it, that's what it was. An overwhelming physical need that sprouted, hoary and demanding, whenever he was around her.

He had nothing to offer her. Nothing. He was empty inside. What love there still was belonged to Andrea. The rest, what a man should feel for a woman, just wasn't there.

And she deserved more.

When Marissa walked into the living room twenty minutes later, Alec was gone. She knew he would be, although she had hoped otherwise.

Marissa let out a long sigh and shook her head. Maybe she was being an idiot, putting herself through all this. But Alec was the first man she had cared about since Antonio.

Maybe even, she amended, the first real man she'd ever cared about, period. Real men knew about the sacrifices that love demanded, that love needed. And Alec had pledged his heart once to a woman who was no longer there. He'd remained faithful to that pledge.

She had to respect him for his decision.

If only she didn't feel as if she literally bloomed whenever he was near her. As if she needed to feel the touch of his hand on her skin, or his eyes on hers to go on existing.

Fresh tears rose, melding into her lashes like unshed diamonds. She was only fooling herself. This wasn't a situation that could continue indefinitely. One way or another, it was going to have to be resolved.

Tears slid down her cheeks as she walked out. Optimist or not, Marissa had a sinking feeling she knew how it would ultimately be resolved.

Alec had kept his distance.

It wasn't hard. Work would have practically consumed him if he allowed it. Every time he turned around, there was something else demanding his attention, his expertise. With Maxwell's new backing, the company was expanding so rapidly, it was a struggle just keeping up. He certainly felt as if he needed a break.

But there was no way he could get a respite. If he left some of the madness behind and worked out of the house, she would be there, singing to the children, cooking, taking care of the house, him and every detail in his life with such an effortlessness that he would get comfortable again.

And he knew where that would lead. To a fatal mistake.

The one he had almost made before his daughter had inadvertently rescued him.

Rex thought that he was lucky, having someone like Marissa in his life. Alec didn't feel lucky. He felt tortured.

Rex popped into the corner office to see if Alec was still there. Disbelief and disapproval crisscrossed his furrowed brow as he entered.

Rex leaned a hip against the drawing table. If Alec didn't take the cake, he didn't know who did.

"Personally, I think you're an idiot. Brilliant," Rex qualified when Alec looked up at him sharply, "but an idiot."

Alec rubbed the bridge of his nose. He had been staring at the same screen now for fifteen minutes and his eyes were tired. His head was throbbing, making him irritable. "And to what do I owe this assessment?"

Alec had never been able to play dumb very well. "You know damn well what you owe it to." Rex leaned forward, getting closer to his friend, though his voice filled the entire room. "You've got a gorgeous woman in your house and you don't do anything about it."

The chair squeaked as Alec leaned back. Just what he needed, someone else to tell him how to live his life. "And what do you propose I do about it?"

Rex threw up his hands. "At the very least, sleep with her."

This was going to be a dead-end conversation. Alec didn't need or want any more advice from anyone. "How do you know I don't?"

Rex snorted. "Because I know you. You're so damn honorable, you don't believe in one-night stands." A sly look slipped over his wide features. "Although her particular stand deserves at least a month's dallying, if not more."

Alec could feel his temper simmering. "That's enough, Rex."

Rex spread his hands in mock innocence. "Hey, if she were in my house, I'd certainly avail myself of what she has to offer. Why don't you?"

Dark brows touched over the bridge of his nose as Alec scowled at the man he considered his friend. His voice was steely, dangerous. "I said, that's enough, Rex."

Rex smiled in triumph, the lecherous look leaving his face as if it had never existed. "Yes, I do believe it is."

Giving up, Alec abandoned the computer screen altogether. He turned his chair around to face Rex squarely. "What the hell are you talking about?"

"An experiment," Rex answered mildly. "I just proved my point."

Alec was in no mood for playing any games. His temper was just about rubbed raw. "Which is?"

"That you're in love with her."

Alec stared at Rex for a second, stunned, before he finally found his voice. "You're crazy."

"No, but you are," Rex insisted seriously, "if you screw this up and let Marissa get away." He saw Alec opening his mouth to protest, and continued quickly. "In the last two weeks, you've been spending more time here than Joe and me put together." And there was only one reason for it. "You're hiding."

"I'm working." This was ridiculous. He didn't have time to defend himself like this. Had Rex gone completely crazy? "Hey, you're the one who keeps telling me we need all this—" exasperated, Alec gestured at the piles on his desk "—done yesterday."

It was an excuse and they both knew it. "Yes, but it's my job to run around like a chicken without a head." They'd had so-called crises before and Alec had never practically lived in the office. He was too much of a family man for that. "You're supposed to be like Scotty on the *Enterprise* and tell me that you 'Canna do it, cap'n.'"

Rex rendered probably what would have gone down as the worst impression of the popular character in history. Alec would have laughed at it if he weren't so annoyed with him.

"And then you work a miracle or two and get it done. But not immediately. Take some time, breathe. We set up a workstation for you at home, for God's sake. Use it," Rex ordered.

He didn't need Rex to remind him of the workstation at home. Home was where his problem was.

"I do," he growled.

"Yeah. On Wednesdays, when she's at class." Rex knew all about her classes. Under prodding, Alec had told him a few things about Marissa the Monday after the party.

"That was my arrangement with her," he said coldly.

He could give him a whole list of reasons if he wanted, but Rex wasn't taken in by any of it. "Did you also 'arrange' to be hiding from her the rest of the time?"

Though it hurt his head to look at the screen, Alec did, afraid that if he continued to look at Rex, he was going to punch him out. "You have no idea what you're talking about."

Rex swung the chair around so that Alec was forced to look at him. Arms on either side of the chair, he leaned in until he was literally in Alec's face, where he intended to remain until he talked sense into him.

"Yes, I do," he said, growing serious. "I'm talking about one of my best friends turning into a hollow shell of a man when he has a chance not to." He sighed. "For some, Alec, love doesn't happen at all. For others, they get lucky once. And a very rare few get lucky twice. You've got a lottery ticket in your hand, buddy. Are you going to use it, or tear it up?"

"I'm going to finish my work." Gripping both wrists,

he removed Rex's hands from the armrests and turned his chair back to face the desk.

"You're fired," Rex said to the back of Alec's head. "Go home."

Alec didn't even bother turning around to look at Rex. He started playing with a set of coordinates on the screen. The shape altered. Distorted, actually. Damn it all. "You can't fire me, Rex. I have part interest in the company."

"All right, then I'm relieving you of duty and putting you on the sick list."

Back to the "Star Trek" metaphor, Alec thought with a heavy sigh. It had been Rex's consuming passion throughout college. He'd never been able to get into it himself. "I'm not sick."

"Mental illness is considered a sickness. And you're acting like a loon."

Alec pressed the Escape button and the screen turned blank. It was late. He wasn't going to get anything more done tonight. He'd used up what little creativity he seemed to have available hours ago.

He frowned at Rex, resigned. "You're not going to shut up, are you?"

Rex shook his head, a smug look creasing his lips. "Nope."

Alec reached for the telephone. "I'm going to get Joe over here to haul you out on the carpet and get you to stop harassing me."

Rex placed his hand on top of Alec's on the receiver. "Joe's backing me on this, Alec. He got a good eyeful of Marissa at the party, too. And we both saw you together."

Alec felt like a petulant kid, but he was tired. "Doesn't prove anything."

"You're in denial," Rex observed. He thought for a minute, trying to remember. "Don't you at least have a class to go to? That Kid and Me thing?"

"Baby and Me," Alec corrected. "And I can't make it. It's too late." Class was long over.

"Do I have to carry you out? Alec, go home. Go home to your daughter, to your life. Don't look back years from now and say, 'Damn, but Rex was a smart man. I really should have listened to him.'"

Alec laughed, too tired to protest anymore. "That is never going to happen." Shutting off his computer, he rose to his feet. "But because I can't stand listening to you anymore, I am going to leave."

"One way or another, doesn't matter to me. As long as you go."

Chapter Twelve

The house was quiet when he let himself in. Almost too quiet. Alec looked around. There wasn't a thing out of place. It was hard to imagine that this was the personal play area of two energetic toddlers during the day.

Whatever might have gone on here earlier, it was all quiet and neat now. Quiet and neat. Things he had been taking for granted lately.

He'd been taking a lot of things for granted lately, he thought as he walked into the kitchen. And they all had to do with Marissa.

Opening the refrigerator, Alec took a can of soda from the rack in the door and tugged on the metal ring. As it fizzed, he took a long, deep pull, shutting the refrigerator door with his elbow. A vague sense of hunger registered, but he decided to ignore it, too tired to fix himself something.

He looked toward the table. There was a covered dish sitting at the place he customarily sat. Alec shook his head. She was always one step ahead of him.

Straddling the chair, he lifted the lid from the plate. There were several pieces of fried chicken on it, cold now. But it was good hot or cold.

Just like her, he mused. Whether she was being passionate, or just amusing and witty, Marissa whet his appetite.

He picked up a piece of chicken and began to eat, his mind on the woman in the rooms above the garage.

Was he going to continue to do that? To just think about her, to just look and never do anything more about it?

He thought of what Rex had said to him. All of it. Much as he hated to admit it, Rex did have a point. So what was he going to do? Was he going to use his lottery ticket or just tear it up?

Alec didn't know. He really didn't know.

He concentrated on filling the void in his belly, ignoring the much larger one that loomed before him in his life. He didn't have to make any decisions tonight, not when he was too tired to really think straight.

As if thinking straight actually helped.

Alec finished the meal and put the dish in the dishwasher. It was empty. She'd put everything away. Frustrated, though he really wouldn't have been able to explain why, Alec tossed the empty soda can into the bag Marissa kept for recycling.

How the hell did she manage to be so damn efficient? How could she just go on with her life at top speed when he felt as if he was suddenly stuck in mud, unable to move forward, unable to move back into the sterile life he'd had before she came? Wasn't she as bothered about this impasse they found themselves in as he was?

Apparently not. She was functioning. Brilliantly, while he…he felt as if his wheels were just spinning in place in that damn tar pit.

Why not? It was his problem, not hers. She'd probably already moved on in her mind. But not him. No, not him.

Why not him? he demanded of himself. He'd been the one to set down the terms, say he couldn't handle loving and losing again. So he had chosen not to love at all and she had accepted that.

Easy for her.

Hard for him.

He was making himself crazy. What he needed right now was not answers to his riddles, but sleep. Pure, simple sleep.

Alec started up the stairs to his room. He was dead tired in more ways than one. And, like as not, probably facing another sleepless night. They'd all been pretty much sleepless since the night of the costume party.

Since the night he'd almost taken her and hadn't.

Midway up, Alec thought he heard something downstairs. Maybe it was just what was left of his flagging imagination, but it bore checking out. Maybe Marissa had forgotten to turn off one of the baby monitors downstairs.

He went back to the kitchen. There was no monitor there, on or otherwise. She must have moved it, he decided. He was too tired to care where. But as he turned from the kitchen, he found himself walking toward the spare bedroom. The room where she worked on her thesis. He hadn't the faintest idea why. Maybe it was just basic instinct.

Or maybe he just wanted to be in a room where she had been recently.

The door was closed, just as it usually was. But there was a light peering out from beneath it, spilling out over the sill. As he listened, he heard the sound of keys being struck rapidly.

She was still in the house. A flicker of hope rose within him.

Alec picked up his hand to knock on the door, then decided against it. What was he going to say to her once she opened the door? He hadn't the foggiest idea. She'd always been so easy to talk to, even before he actually knew her. Now he couldn't find the right words to use.

Sighing, he turned from the door.

It opened and suddenly she was there, looking up at him quizzically, cutting off his silent escape.

So she hadn't conjured him up just now, the way she'd done at least a dozen times since he had all but gone into exile. He actually was home.

Big deal. Anger nudged aside the momentary ray of excitement that pierced her.

Marissa pasted a smile on her face, the same one she'd always used when she'd been determined not to show the Sergeant that his critical words had cut deep.

"I thought I heard something. Been home long?" Turning, Marissa crossed back to the desk.

Alec shook his head. "No. Just a little while." Damn, but he felt awkward. It shouldn't be this way. "The chicken was good."

"Even better warm." She couldn't help the slight dig. Where the hell had he been all these days? "But cold chicken's all right." She sat down at the computer and looked at the screen. Suddenly unable to concentrate, her mind turned blank.

Common sense, Alec thought, would have had him leaving, especially since he felt as uncomfortable as a man who'd gone out in his underwear to get the morning paper, only to have the door slam shut behind him.

Instead, Alec found himself drifting into the room. He hadn't been inside it since he'd set up the computer for her.

She had the baby monitors set up on either side of the screen, like twin speakers. Set to different frequencies, there was one for each of the nurseries. Always on call, he mused. What was he doing, cutting someone like that out of his life? Maybe he really was crazy.

Searching for something to say, Alec nodded at the computer screen. "How's it going?"

Remarkably, considering the state of Marissa's mind these last few days, the thesis was coming together rather well. Her advisor in the department was pleased. Everyone, it seemed, was pleased with her. Except the one person who counted.

"It's almost done." He'd hardly been around for the past two weeks and she had longed for the sight of him, but now that he was here, she found that she couldn't look at him. She didn't want him to see the pain that was in her heart. Marissa was sure he'd see it in her eyes.

It was a matter of preserving what little pride she had left to her.

"Which is a good thing," she continued. "The deadline's breathing down my neck. I'll be glad to see it finished." Marissa slanted a look toward him. "All of it."

"All of it?" He wasn't sure he got her meaning.

He was afraid that he did.

"Going to class, rushing around." She gathered together the hard copy of the revisions she had printed tonight. "I'm graduating in less than a month." Marissa looked speculatively at the pages in her hands. "Provided that the committee reviewing this likes my thesis."

He wasn't accustomed to seeing uncertainty in her eyes. "They'll like it."

"How would you know? Maybe it's garbage." She frowned at the screen, her mind frozen. Maybe she should just call it quits for tonight. There was no use pushing it.

She was serious, he realized. "Nothing you put your hand to is ever garbage."

Marissa smiled absently, knowing Alec was just paying lip service. He didn't mean what he said. If he was untrue to the sentiments she had felt in his kiss, how could she believe anything he said? "I don't know, this might come close."

He came around to stand behind her and looked at the screen. Slowly the words faded and the screen saver he had programmed for her came on. She was there, looking back at him, smiling the way he remembered her. The way she wasn't now.

"Do you really believe that?"

Marissa shrugged. She waited until the photo of her son reformed into her face again, then struck a key, bringing back her thesis. "Maybe I'm too close."

"Want me to read it?" he offered. "Tell you what I think?"

She couldn't help the accusation that rose into her eyes. He'd used the excuse of a busy schedule to keep him at the office and away from both home and the classes he was supposed to be taking with Andrea. Now, suddenly, he had time to read her thesis? "When would you have the time?"

She was angry at him. He could hear it in her voice. Alec couldn't really blame her. "Maybe I could scrounge some up."

Marissa didn't want any favors, any crumbs tossed in her direction. She'd already humiliated herself enough for one lifetime when it came to him. "That's all right, don't trouble yourself. After all, you're very busy."

She was distant, almost disinterested. Well, what the hell had he expected? For her to remain the way she'd been, warm and friendly, while he flip-flopped from Jekyll to Hyde and back again at will?

Her manner had him taking stock of how the immediate future would be affected by her graduation. Something he hadn't thought about up until now. "Once you graduate, what then?"

She'd thought about this long and hard. Her answer was

different now than it would have been two weeks ago. More on track with what it had been before she had come here.

"Then I go job hunting. I have a few prospects." She thought of the telephone call she'd taken yesterday. "There's a clinic that's responded favorably to my application. If we like each other, I might go to work for them."

He was losing her, he thought. Really losing her. "You'd be working there full-time?"

She raised her eyes to his. He couldn't read anything there. She was deliberately shutting him out. "Yes."

Alec took a breath. "That means you'll be moving out?"

She nodded. She couldn't tell if that even bothered him. "I'll be able to afford my own place again. A real home for Christopher," she added. "Don't worry, I won't leave you in a lurch," she assured him. If he was concerned about this change at all, it was only because he was probably afraid she'd leave him without any help. "There's still time to find a replacement."

He felt oddly numbed, like a man who'd been submerged in freezing water. "I guess I had better get around to conducting interviews again."

Alec waited for her to say something—anything—that would let him know the door between them wasn't completely shut.

"Yes," she agreed, her voice tight. "I guess you'd better."

He didn't know what to do with himself. He just knew he didn't want to remain standing here, looking like a fool.

"You probably want to get back to work." Alec backed out of the room. His hand curled around the doorknob. "I'll see you in the morning."

"See you," Marissa murmured in response, not looking up. It was only after she heard the door close that she dared look in his direction. "You big, dumb jerk," she added, tears rising in her eyes.

* * *

He'd been right.

It was another sleepless night. And what little sleep he did get was littered with dreams, dreams of Marissa. They were all the same. She was walking away from him. Over and over again.

All he had to do was one thing, and she wouldn't go. He knew that, sensed it, yet he couldn't think what that one thing was.

And so she left. Again and again, through the course of the entire night. Every time he closed his eyes and fell asleep, there she was, walking away, out of his life. Forever.

Well, he'd better get used to it, he thought when he finally got out of bed the next morning. It was going to happen soon enough.

Alec was halfway through a briefing he was conducting that afternoon when he decided with resounding finality that he didn't want to get used to it. Didn't want to get used to life without her.

And he thought he knew what he had to do to make her stay.

The realization that he was probably the biggest fool to have ever walked the face of the earth washed over Alec like a huge wave crashing down on an unsuspecting surfer. It stopped him in midsentence.

Alec looked from Rex to Joe, not even seeing the other assistants who were seated around the table. He knew what he had to do.

"I've got to leave," he said abruptly, backing away from the huge screen he'd been using to illustrate the finer points of the program.

Rex exchanged looks with Joe. Joe looked bewildered, but Rex was smiling to himself. Finally.

"What did you say?" Joe stared at Alec as if he thought he'd heard wrong.

Alec glanced at his notes on the table, then decided to leave them where they were. Rex could use them to conduct the rest of the briefing. He looked at his watch, even though he had just looked at it less than a minute ago. "I said I have to leave. I've got a Baby and Me class to get to."

Joe waved around at the table. "Now? Alec, we're in the middle of a meeting. A meeting you're conducting."

Alec looked to Rex for support. "Nothing you can't handle without me."

Rex nodded, already reaching for the notes. "We'll muddle through it, don't worry. Just get moving. And by the way, it's about time!"

Alec didn't answer. He didn't even hear Rex as he ran down the hall to the elevator. He had fifteen minutes to get to class.

It took him twenty. Even then, he'd only made it by watching his rearview mirror for signs of approaching police vehicles as he drove faster than was allowed, barring a life and death emergency.

He figured this qualified.

There was no parking available in the lot when he pulled up in it, except at the very perimeter. Alec raced all the way from his car to the building, and then to class.

Breathing heavily, he hurried in. The door slipped from his fingers, slamming in his wake and drawing everyone's attention to his entrance.

Marissa swung around. When she saw him, her first thought was that there was something wrong. But it couldn't have to do with either of the children, they were with her. She couldn't think of any other reason Alec would come running in, dressed as if he had just dashed out of a meeting.

Before she could ask, he was at her side, taking her arm. He didn't even say hello.

"Excuse me." Alec nodded at the woman Marissa had just been talking to. "But I have to talk to Marissa."

The woman looked at them, a bemused expression on her face. Marissa was painfully aware that every pair of eyes was focused on them as Alec dragged her out into the hallway.

Adrenaline up, she didn't know what to think. "Alec, what's wrong?"

He didn't answer until the door closed behind them and he was sure they were alone.

"What's wrong?" he repeated. "What's wrong is that I hate conducting interviews."

Her mouth dropped open. What was he, crazy? "You dragged me out of class to tell me that?" she demanded incredulously.

Marissa didn't know whether to punch him or just ignore him and walk away. She struggled to keep hold of her temper. She'd never known she even had one, until he had entered her life. Of all the selfish, self-centered jerks, he took the prize.

She blew out a breath, curbing the desire to tell him exactly what she thought of him. "I'll help you, all right?"

Marissa turned to reenter the class, only to have Alec take hold of her arm and swing her back around to face him again. "No, it's not all right."

What did he want from her? Blood? "Then I'll do them for you." She clenched her teeth together. "Now, can I get back to class?"

Shifting, he barred her way back into the room. "You really want to help? Then don't go."

He really was an egotist, wasn't he? How could she have been so blind as to fall in love with this man? He didn't care about her feelings, only convenience.

She fisted her hands at her waist. "You want me to continue being Andrea's nanny? Is that what you want?"

It was a trite saying, but she really was magnificent when she was angry. He'd never realized just how magnificent.

"No."

He had completely lost her now. "Then what do you want? Help me out here, Alec." Sarcasm and confusion mingled in her voice. "What do you want?"

His eyes touched her face, her hair. God, but he had missed seeing her. Missed her so much that it hurt. He hadn't fully realized it until this very minute.

"You."

"Me," she repeated, dumbfounded.

For a second she wavered, wanting more than anything else in the world to believe him. Knowing it was a mistake if she did. He didn't mean what she wanted him to. He was just talking about her presence in his home. She'd made things too easy for him and now he didn't want them to change.

She gave it to him with both barrels. "It's a little late for that, Alec. If you haven't noticed—and why should you, you're never around—I've been hardening my heart. It's not easy—" now *there* was an understatement "—but I'm getting there. I have a life to think of. Two. Mine and Christopher's. I owe him the best future I can come up with so that he can have one, too."

Because he couldn't stand here another moment and not touch her, he ran his hands along her arms. When she shrugged them off, he placed them on her shoulders. There was no way he was going to let her shrug him out of her life.

"I know. But I'm not asking you not to have a career, Marissa. I was just hoping you could combine the two."

He was deliberately being obscure to confuse her. Well,

she was through being confused. Through wanting what she couldn't have. From now on, she was going to be a realist.

"What, being a child psychologist and a nanny?" Marissa shook her head. That wasn't possible, not anymore. "I don't—"

"No," he corrected her quietly. "A child psychologist and a wife."

He could say what he wanted, it wasn't going to change anything. "Look, I know that these interviews are—a wife?" She looked at him. She couldn't have heard right. "Whose wife?"

For the first time, he allowed himself to smile. "Mine."

What was he talking about? He'd made such a production out of telling her that it just wasn't meant to be between them. "How can I be your wife?"

"Well, first there are blood tests, then—"

She wasn't going to get waylaid with double talk, not this time. "You didn't ask me."

He searched her eyes, looking for her answer. The right answer. "I'm asking now."

To say she was surprised wouldn't have begun to cover it. "Just like that?"

"No, not just like that." He slowly combed his fingers through her hair. He'd almost lost her. The thought chilled his heart. "After a lot of anguish and soul searching."

Had it been that hard for him to find a place for her? "Boy, you'll do anything not to conduct those interviews, won't you?"

This wasn't about interviews, or nannies, or anything else but him and her. And what they had together. "No, I'll do anything not to lose you. The way I almost did." He was risking everything, putting himself on the line. But to win everything, you have to risk losing it. He knew that now. "Marissa, you have every right to say no, but I'm hoping that you won't."

"And you're not afraid anymore?" She tried to read his eyes. "Of what's down the road?"

He wouldn't lie to her, even if it meant losing her. "Yeah, I am. But I'm more afraid of walking down that road without you. You were right, you know."

Yes, she knew. But she needed to hear him say it. "About?"

He thought for a moment, wanting to get the words straight. "About having a little bit of something wonderful being better than having a whole lot of nothing. I started thinking about what it would be like without you. Really without you, not just because I was holed up at the office, but because when I came home, you wouldn't be there."

She was trying to hold it at bay, but golden rays of sunshine were beginning to prod their way forward, seeking to capture her heart. "And?"

He pulled her into his arms. Where she belonged. "And I didn't like it."

"You'd get used to it." She had no intentions of letting him, but she wanted to hear his response.

"I don't want to get used to it." He kissed her forehead softly, then each eye. He felt his pulse rate accelerating. "I'm already used to you. I don't take to change very well. I want you in my life, Marissa. And in Andrea's. I love you and I want you to marry me. I want both you and Christopher to marry Andrea and me."

A family of her own. A real family. Complete in every way. It didn't get any better than this.

"When?" she breathed.

"How does graduation day sound? That way, we'll both have something to celebrate. You'll have your degree. And I'll have you." He pressed a kiss to her throat.

He made it hard to think when he did that. It took her a second to answer. "It sounds like you're ready to make a commitment."

"I already have." He looked into her eyes, pledging her his heart. "To love you for as long as you let me."

Her smile was wide, drawing him inside. "Then I guess you're in it for the long haul."

Alec brought his mouth down to hers. "I certainly hope so."

*   *   *   *   *

In April 1997
Bestselling Author

DALLAS SCHULZE

takes her Family Circle series to new heights with

In April 1997 Dallas Schulze brings readers a
brand-new, longer, out-of-series title featuring the
characters from her popular Family Circle miniseries.

When rancher Keefe Walker found Tessa Wyndham he
knew that she needed a man's protection—she was
pregnant, alone and on the run from a heartless past.
Keefe was also hiding from a dark past...but in one
overwhelming moment he and Tessa forged a family
bond that could never be broken.

Available in April wherever books are sold.

Look us up on-line at: http://www.romance.net

DSST

Take 4 bestselling love stories FREE

Plus get a FREE surprise gift!

Special Limited-time Offer

Mail to Silhouette Reader Service™

3010 Walden Avenue
P.O. Box 1867
Buffalo, N.Y. 14240-1867

YES! Please send me 4 free Silhouette Romance™ novels and my free surprise gift. Then send me 6 brand-new novels every month, which I will receive months before they appear in bookstores. Bill me at the low price of $2.67 each plus 25¢ delivery and applicable sales tax, if any.* That's the complete price and a savings of over 10% off the cover prices—quite a bargain! I understand that accepting the books and gift places me under no obligation ever to buy any books. I can always return a shipment and cancel at any time. Even if I never buy another book from Silhouette, the 4 free books and the surprise gift are mine to keep forever.

215 BPA A3UT

Name _____ (PLEASE PRINT) _____

Address _____ Apt. No. _____

City _____ State _____ Zip _____

This offer is limited to one order per household and not valid to present Silhouette Romance™ subscribers. *Terms and prices are subject to change without notice. Sales tax applicable in N.Y.

USROM-696   ©1990 Harlequin Enterprises Limited

As seen on TV!
Free Gift Offer

With a Free Gift proof-of-purchase from any Silhouette® book,
you can receive a beautiful cubic zirconia pendant.

This gorgeous marquise-shaped stone is a genuine cubic
zirconia—accented by an 18" gold tone necklace.

(Approximate retail value $19.95)

Send for yours today...
compliments of ▼ *Silhouette*®
TM

To receive your free gift, a cubic zirconia pendant, send us one original proof-of-
purchase, photocopies not accepted, from the back of any Silhouette Romance™,
Silhouette Desire®, Silhouette Special Edition®, Silhouette Intimate Moments®
or Silhouette Yours Truly™ title available in February, March and April at your favorite
retail outlet, together with the Free Gift Certificate, plus a check or money order for
$1.65 u.s./$2.15 can. (do not send cash) to cover postage and handling, payable
to Silhouette Free Gift Offer. We will send you the specified gift. Allow 6 to 8 weeks for
delivery. Offer good until April 30, 1997 or while quantities last. Offer valid in the
U.S. and Canada only.

Free Gift Certificate

Name: _____

Address: _____

City: _____ State/Province: _____ Zip/Postal Code: _____

Mail this certificate, one proof-of-purchase and a check or money order for postage
and handling to: SILHOUETTE FREE GIFT OFFER 1997. In the U.S.: 3010 Walden
Avenue, P.O. Box 9077, Buffalo NY 14269-9077. In Canada: P.O. Box 613, Fort Erie,
Ontario L2Z 5X3.

FREE GIFT OFFER   084-KFD
ONE PROOF-OF-PURCHASE
To collect your fabulous FREE GIFT, a cubic zirconia pendant, you must include this
original proof-of-purchase for each gift with the properly completed Free Gift Certificate.

084-KFD

Also by bestselling author
MARIE FERRARELLA

Silhouette Special Edition®

#09892	BABY IN THE MIDDLE	$3.50 U.S. ☐ /$3.99 CAN.☐
#09931	HUSBAND: SOME ASSEMBLY REQUIRED	$3.50 U.S. ☐
		$3.99 CAN. ☐
#23997	BABY'S FIRST CHRISTMAS*	$3.75 U.S. ☐ /$4.25 CAN.☐

Silhouette Romance®

#19078	FATHER IN THE MAKING	$2.99 U.S. ☐ /$3.50 CAN.☐
#19096	THE WOMEN IN JOE SULLIVAN'S LIFE	$2.99 U.S. ☐
		$3.50 CAN. ☐

Silhouette Intimate Moments®

#07661	CAITLIN'S GUARDIAN ANGEL	$3.75 U.S. ☐ /$4.25 CAN.☐
#07686	HAPPY NEW YEAR—BABY!*	$3.75 U.S. ☐ /$4.25 CAN.☐

Silhouette Desire®

#05988	HUSBAND: OPTIONAL*	$3.50 U.S. ☐ /$3.99 CAN.☐

Silhouette Yours Truly®

#52013	THE 7lb., 2oz. VALENTINE*	$3.50 U.S. ☐ /$3.99 CAN.☐
#52019	LET'S GET MOMMY MARRIED	$3.50 U.S. ☐ /$3.99 CAN.☐

*MARIE FERRARELLA'S bestselling miniseries "The Baby of the Month Club"
(Limited quantities available)

TOTAL AMOUNT		$_____
POSTAGE & HANDLING		$_____
($1.00 for one book, 50¢ for each additional)		
APPLICABLE TAXES*		$_____
TOTAL PAYABLE		$_____
(check or money order—please do not send cash)		

To order, send the completed form, along with a check or money order for the total above, payable to Silhouette Books, to: **In the U.S.:** 3010 Walden Avenue, P.O. Box 9077, Buffalo, NY 14269-9077; **In Canada:** P.O. Box 636, Fort Erie, Ontario, L2A 5X3.

Name:_____

Address:_____ _____

State/Prov.:_____ Zip/Postal Code:_____

*New York residents remit applicable sales taxes.
Canadian residents remit applicable GST and provincial taxes.   SMFBACK

Silhouette®

Look us up on-line at: http://www.romance.net

IN CELEBRATION OF MOTHER'S DAY, JOIN
SILHOUETTE THIS MAY AS WE BRING YOU

a funny thing
HAPPENED ON THE WAY TO THE
DELIVERY ROOM

THESE THREE STORIES, CELEBRATING THE
LIGHTER SIDE OF MOTHERHOOD, ARE
WRITTEN BY YOUR FAVORITE AUTHORS:

KASEY MICHAELS
KATHLEEN EAGLE
EMILIE RICHARDS

When three couples make the trip to the delivery
room, they get more than their own bundles of
joy...they get the promise of love!

Available this May,
wherever Silhouette books are sold.

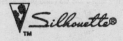

Look us up on-line at: http://www.romance.net   MD

Silhouette Romance proudly invites you
to get to know the members of

The Single Daddy Club

a new miniseries by award-winning author
Donna Clayton

Derrick: Ex-millitary man who unexpectedly
falls into fatherhood
MISS MAXWELL BECOMES A MOM (March '97)

Jason: Widowed daddy desperately in need of some live-in help
NANNY IN THE NICK OF TIME (April '97)

Reece: Single and satisfied father of one about
to meet his Ms. Right
BEAUTY AND THE BACHELOR DAD (May '97)

Don't miss any of these heartwarming stories as
three single dads say bye-bye to their bachelor days.
Only from

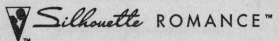

Silhouette ROMANCE™

Look us up on-line at: http://www.romance.net   SDC1

twins
on the doorstep
by Stella Bagwell

When the Murdock sisters found abandoned twins
on their ranch-house doorstep, they had no clue the
little ones would lead them to love!

Come see how each sister meets her match—and how
the twins' family is discovered—in

THE SHERIFF'S SON (SR #1218, April 1997)

THE RANCHER'S BRIDE (SR #1224, May 1997)

THE TYCOON'S TOTS (SR #1228, June 1997)

TWINS ON THE DOORSTEP—a brand-new miniseries
by Stella Bagwell starting in April...
Only from

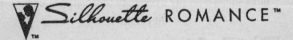 ROMANCE™

Look us up on-line at: http://www.romance.net   TWINS1